With
Little Help
from My Friends

Carolyn Addie

Copyright © 2022 Carolyn Addie
All rights reserved
First Edition

PAGE PUBLISHING
Conneaut Lake, PA

First originally published by Page Publishing 2022

ISBN 978-1-6624-6677-9 (pbk)
ISBN 978-1-6624-6678-6 (digital)

Printed in the United States of America

Donovan Joseph
Forever our Special Angel

We'll hold you in our hearts until we hold you in heaven

Contents

Introduction..7

1	Run for Your Life...9
2	You Really Got a Hold on Me............................13
3	Step Inside Love..17
4	Don't Pass Me By..21
5	Glad All Over..25
6	Getting Better...29
7	Magical Mystery Tour...33
8	Here Comes the Sun!..39
9	I'll Follow the Sun..43
10	A Taste of Honey..45
11	All You Need Is Love..51
12	Act Naturally..55
13	Nothin' Shakin'...57
14	Baby's in Black..61
15	Ticket to Ride...65
16	It's Only Love...69
17	Baby It's You...73
18	Come Together...77
19	Twist and Shout..81
20	You Never Give Me Your Money........................85
21	Come and Get It!..89
22	Ooh! My Soul...93
23	Sexy Sadie...97
24	You Like Me Too Much....................................101
25	A Shot of Rhythm and Blues............................103
26	You've Got to Hide Your Love Away................107
27	A Day in the Life..109
28	Lonesome Tears in My Eyes.............................115
29	Crying, Waiting, Hoping..................................119
30	A Beginning...123

Answers in Chapters...127
Song Titles in Alphabetical Order..135

Introduction

With a Little Help from My Friends is an uplifting story that opens the "eye" to a world where peace and love exist. It begins one morning when the main character awakens from her peaceful dream and cannot muster the energy to face another day in our troubled world. At last, she escapes back into her golden slumbers, only to be awakened by some three-eyed miniature creatures. They whisk her from her bed and swiftly guide her into their spacecraft, The Glass Onion. She feels frightened and confused but believes she must still be dreaming. As the flight continues, she soon becomes mesmerized by the loving nature of the jovial characters. Once arriving on Savoy Truffle, she's welcomed by hundreds more of the three-eyed friendly Abelets. Her spirit cautiously awakens, and her fears begin to diminish as she becomes energized by her new friends. The bonds of friendship grow deeper and deeper while sharing many adventures, and eventually she learns why she was selected as their *Chosen One*. Throughout her eye-opening travels, she wonders whether she drifted back into her world of dreams or if her new friends drifted into her world of reality. In the end, she uncovers the truth.

This fun-loving tale unites over three hundred Fab Four Song Titles into a heartwarming story for all ages, hoping to spark the desire to bring love into the forefront of our lives.

From me to you, enjoy the ride!

Chapter One

Run for Your Life

MY PEACEFUL DREAM SUDDENLY ENDED WHEN I was awakened by the crashing sounds of thunder. As I listened to the raindrops splatter against my window, angry flashes of light illuminated the sky. I closed my eyes, attempting to return to my dream, but after countless tries, it just proved hopeless. While lying motionless, never-ending thoughts of our troubled world consumed me. I thought, if only there was a magic wand that could take away our sorrow and misery, we could live in a world where kindness reigns and love triumphs. After all, we are here only once; there is not a second time. My thoughts began running wild, and being a well-known paperback writer, I considered climbing out of bed to write them down, but I quickly changed my mind after hearing the rumbling turbulence outside. I pulled the covers over my head and tried once more to resume my dream, but all my efforts proved to be in vain. It was time to face the dismal day, but it felt as though some invisible chains were holding me captive. Therefore, my world had no other choice but to wait for me. I buried my face in my pillow, and at last, those beautiful golden slumbers showed up and rescued me.

There was no telling how much time passed before my dream was rudely interrupted by some strange creatures appearing at my bedside. Within a split second, they whisked me from my bed, out of my window, and into a hovering spaceship. Feeling terrified and confused, I began pinching myself over and over to wake up, but nothing changed. One of the strangers soon grabbed my hand and escorted me to a tiny seat aboard the vessel. If anyone would have asked, "Tell me what you see," I simply would've answered, "I've just seen a face unlike any other in my life." I desperately tried convincing myself, "I'm only sleeping," while my brain was screaming, "Run for your life!" But where would I be running to? My whole world turned upside down in the blink of an eye.

My eyes remained locked on my mysterious captors as I sat paralyzed in my undersized seat. Their facial features were identical to ours on earth, except for an extra eye between their other two. Not one was more than four feet tall, yet each one had their own distinct characteristics. I repeatedly asked myself who these mystifying characters were and why they wanted me. My mind flashed back to the crashing sounds of thunder that awakened me. It was when I had the chance to climb out of bed and write down my thoughts about our troubled world. How I wished it were something I would have done, and maybe, just maybe, I wouldn't be surrounded by some pint-sized creatures in an alien spaceship.

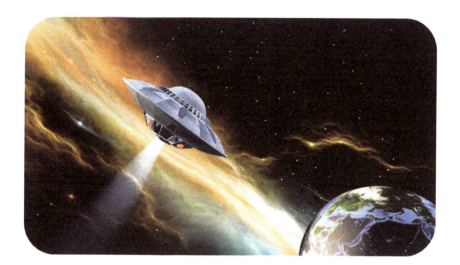

Chapter Two

You Really Got a Hold on Me

THE INSIDE OF THE SHIP WAS JUST as imaginary as all the miniature beings. Name tags were attached to their colorful flamboyant clothes. The stranger who had grabbed my hand to usher me to the vacant seat had Ginor scrawled on his label. His chocolate-brown hair matched his chocolate brown skin, and his welcoming smile gave me the chills. In the far corner sat another stranger named Roggee. His charcoal black hair was highlighted by the multicolored turban sitting on his head, and there seemed to be a genuine shyness about him. Not far away stood the tallest who appeared to be the whimsical character of the bunch. His label read Hojn, and his straight dark hair emphasized his dark almond-shaped eyes. The very last one was wearing a rainbow sombrero, complimenting his smooth bronze skin. His tag read Ulap, and his presence filled the entire vessel with warmth.

Those were the boys, and when I turned around, I saw her standing there, the girl. Her label read Fantebela, and her skin was as white as pearls. Golden hair flowed to her shoulders, and unpredictably, our eyes affectionately bonded. For some odd reason, having another female on the vessel was comforting, but when I finally spoke, "Thank you girl for being here," to my sheer disappointment, there was no response.

Fantebela clung to Ulap's side like a magnet, and they were speaking in a language that was clearly foreign to me. Yet when hearing the words ob-la-di, ob-la-da, there was no mistaken that they were words of love. Soon after, Ulap walked over and buckled my seat belt as if I were a little child. Although I was feeling somewhat secure being buckled in, the fact remained, there was no way out. The hovering ship began accelerating up and up, and I knew it was time to brace myself for whatever my future held for me. With much courage, I peered out my window into the vast universe and whispered, "Hello, goodbye," to the barely visible earth I once called home.

    The abstract noise of the motor produced a rhythmic tune with vocal-like pitches sounding like a three-part harmony. The madness of it all heightened to a new level as we continued to soar up and up, but surprisingly, it started to soothe me. Knowing there was no way out, I shouted, "You really got a hold on me!" But to my frustration, there was no reply. Ironically, I was the only one in captivity while each one of them was as free as a bird. I tried to muster up the strength by believing that everything would make sense when I get home.

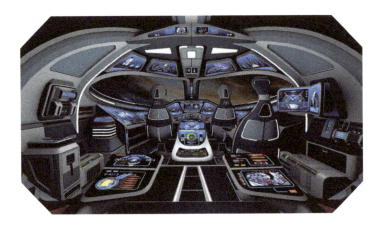

The atmosphere in the vessel exploded with pure energy. Camaraderie seemed to play a major part amongst them as I listened to them laugh in the same language as mine. I continued to explore my surroundings, and it wasn't long before I observed a flickering sign, which read, "Welcome aboard The Glass Onion." A sigh of relief seeing *welcome* was rather calming, yet the reality of it all was beyond my wild imagination. As we soared through space, I needed to hold on for dear life since the time had arrived for whatever my dream or my reality had in store. As I glanced around, full-blown Helter Skelter erupted. Everyone was in perfect synchronization, scrambling all over, reading charts, pushing buttons, and checking every little thing. All over again, my mind spun out of control, believing it's all too much for me to process. The moment had arrived when our downward descent was set in motion. My pinching began again in hopes of waking up, but to no avail. My nerves began to unravel, and it was at that moment Ulap walked his way over to sit beside me. For some unexplained reason, I started babbling, "I want to hold your hand!" He respectfully placed his hand in mine, and within seconds, it was just the two of us. Although my fears had somewhat lessened, the second the ship began to slow down, those same fears began to speed up. As we plummeted downward, I was convinced the echoing sound of the landing gear could be heard back on earth. As the ship came to a screeching halt, so did my heart.

Chapter Three

Step Inside Love

MY HAND REMAINED CLENCHED IN ULAP'S WHEN Fantebela strolled over to unbuckle my seat belt. The three of us made our way to the rear of the ship, where Roggee, Hojn, and Ginor were expecting us. As soon as we arrived, a door creaked opened, and the inner light merged with the outer light. Our eyes were gradually adjusting to the brightness when Fantebela clutched my other hand. In no time, we were floating on white fluffy clouds surrounded by a sapphire sky. An endless marble staircase appeared, and our downward climb began. After almost taking a tumble, Ulap and Fantebela wasted no time holding me closer. As we continued down the steps, a never-ending vision of beauty emerged. Flourishing fields overflowed with flowers in shades of brilliant burgundies, radiant reds, plush purples, glistening greens, and blazing blues. My dream seemed to have spiraled into another dimension, and I asked myself, "Did I just step inside love?" The electrifying feeling intensified as hundreds of tiny people greeted us. They were here, there and everywhere, cheering and waving. Their distinctive characteristics were a sight to behold, and it was no surprise, each had an extra eye. Their soft-spoken words became recognizable the minute I heard, "Good morning good morning!" Why some foreign language was spoken on the spaceship made no sense, but had there been anything so far that did? I politely was returning their smiles when I heard Ulap announce to the crowd, "She's leaving home, so let's make sure our new friend feels welcome." He then turned my way and said, "Let me introduce you. We are the Abelets." My question of *who* they were was answered. But *why* they wanted me was a mystery.

Fantebela and Ulap reached for my hands, and we set off down a scenic trail with all the Abelets parading behind us. Roggee, Ginor, and Hojn were nowhere in sight, and oddly, a sense of sadness fell upon me. Don't ask me why, but I hoped they were somewhere at the rear of the parade. In next to no time, we came upon more flowers showing off their extraordinary brilliance. There were roses, tulips, lilacs, gardenias, orchids, violets, and many others emitting a sweet-smelling aroma. Vegetable gardens overflowed with tomatoes, eggplants, avocados, and watermelons, and their strawberry fields forever literally took my breath away. In the far distance, the sun sparkled over snowcapped mountains and glimmering lakes. Overhead were hundreds of magnificent birds singing like a church choir, and on the ground were hundreds of furry creatures scampering about. Each one enhanced the splendor of their spectacular habitat, which words were powerless to express. Meanwhile, Ulap had been quietly watching me digest my new surroundings. His face lit up as he softly spoke, "Within you without you, the magnificence here will illuminate for lifetimes to come." It was an unusual way to communicate his sentiments, yet I understood his every word. Not a human being on earth could ever fathom the beauty of their breathtaking land. It was a world filled with glorious colors creating a most peaceful inner feeling. There would be no more pinching because, in a strange twist of fate, my new fear was waking up.

Chapter Four

Don't Pass Me By

WITH THE HIGH-SPIRITED ABELETS NOT FAR BEHIND, Fantebela, Ulap, and I followed a cobblestone path onto Blue Jay Way, leading us into a picturesque neighborhood. The sidewalks boasted more beautiful flowers positioned perfectly in front of their pixie-like doors, but not a single soul was around. As we marched along, my imagination began to run wild. A vision of Alice in Wonderland frolicking with her white rabbit popped into view, and when I turned my head, I pictured Snow White and her seven dwarfs strolling down the path, whistling their favorite tune. Just when I thought my harebrained imagination had settled down, I visualized Peter Pan soaring high above after snatching Dorothy and Toto in Kansas City. But my wildest vision of all was witnessing a wicked witch concocting a deadly brew. I imagined she was plotting to fly me away on her disheveled tattered broom. Thank goodness my imagination fizzled when I almost tripped over an old brown shoe. The shoe didn't fit in their picture-perfect neighborhood, but in some crazy way, I did. Although my visions ended, it didn't prevent a most chilling thought from popping into my head; was I to be their next storybook character?

We departed from their neighborhood with all the energetic little people still following us. After arriving in a most charming town, it also was uninhabited, just like their neighborhood. A variety of quaint shops appeared and looked as if they were inviting us to enter. Without any warning, Fantebela and Ulap unpredictably scooted off in front of me. Since they were my only sense of security, those ignored fears of mine started bubbling up. Without me realizing, my shaky voice lifted to a fever-high pitch, "Please don't leave me behind!" They turned and explained that the shop doors were always open and were secretly planning to surprise me with ice cream! With a huge sigh of relief, I shouted out, "Thanks, but please don't pass me by ever again!" They were just as speechless as I was by my words, yet they both respectfully nodded. We then promenaded into the ice cream parlor where Ulap treated himself to the Chipapino ice cream while Fantebela and I double-scooped every single morsel of the Fudgareli. Once I saw her Fudgareli's mustache, my laughter was heard for the first time. My new friend joined me, and in seconds, she concocted a funny face. Little did I know, it was only the beginning of many, many more.

We moseyed along, slurping our ice cream cones, when I observed a sign on one of the shop doors that read "Doctor Robert." Perhaps the Abelets became ill like the Earthlings did? Countless more questions kept resurfacing, but keeping the pace with my new friends had become my top priority. The Abelets were still following in our footsteps, though some had vanished, just like Ginor, Roggee, and Hojn. Naturally, my curiosity peaked as to why *they* also disappeared, but I was much more curious of how my Fudgareli cone tasted so lip-smacking good if I were just dreaming. I decided not to think anymore, at least not until I finished every last bite of my ice cream.

Chapter Five

Glad All Over

AFTER LEAVING THEIR TOWN, WHAT RESEMBLED AN old-fashioned schoolhouse was spotted up ahead. As we approached, I heard a bell clanging away and witnessed a lady who was making all the noise. It was that moment all the children knew playtime had come to its end. Their cheery faces faded as they scampered off the playground, abandoning their swings and slides. Yet those same faces lit up like light bulbs the minute they saw Ulap and Fantebela. A friendly smile surfaced on Ms. Michelle while waving for us to come into the classroom. Meanwhile, our trailing Abelets bolted to the playground, looking like little kids. I guessed they were attempting to turn back time by trying to become youngsters again. My silly thought was perhaps they were hoping to pocket some of that young blood the tiny tykes left behind. I was tempted to join them, but Ms. M was patiently waiting for us at the doorway.

The warmth hovering over us in the classroom created a peaceful atmosphere. Colorful polka dots and stripes were plastered all over their walls and floors. The kids could hardly contain themselves while guiding us to some empty desks. Seeing me trying my best to squeeze into a chair gave all of them a hearty chuckle. As soon as the giggles quieted down, Ms. M cheerfully began to introduce me. Each one had their own individual features, but to no shock, the extra eye. Remarkably, the differences in our appearance did not faze them in the least. Observing their innocence had me question why couldn't we capture that same innocence and hang on to it while growing older and older? They radiated a love that flooded through me like a warm summer breeze. I was feeling happy and glad all over to share such precious moments with such precious children.

We weren't seated long before hearing a pipsqueak's voice cry out, "Can you read us a story, Ms. M?"

She promptly responded, "You must be reading my mind, Teddy boy!" The twins, Layla and Lyric, also chimed in, asking to hear their all-time favorite called *The Escapades of Mr. Kite*. She had read that story numerous times before and asked if everyone was ready to hear it all over again. Fantebela and I giggled when witnessing twenty tiny hands reach sky-high. And so, it was unanimous, Mr. Kite would return to visit the children in the classroom as well as in the story. Surprisingly, all the characters in the story, Mr. Kite, Beethoven, and the neighborhood kids, did not have an extra eye. It crossed my mind that maybe the book was from my planet? Nonetheless, Ms. M just continued reading about how the good-natured Mr. Kite shared his home with his furry lovable dog, Beethoven. The neighborhood cousins, Micaela and Melody would thoughtfully bring him brownies every day, and Mr. Kite would affectionately make them hot chocolate. Their faces would beam watching Mr. Kite's furry best friend perform his amazing tricks. The slobbering would begin after Beethoven obeyed Mr. Kite's commands. "Sit, give me your paw, roll over Beethoven." At first, the kids believed Beethoven was doing all the slobbering, yet the little ones would roar with laughter, knowing the real culprit was Mr. Kite. Once the story ended, one would argue it was the children who received the most satisfaction; however, when it came right down to the nitty-gritty, it was all in being for the benefit of Mr. Kite as he was the true recipient of the greatest pleasure.

Our visit was reaching its end when a sweet, angelic youngster, named Donovan, asked Ms. M to please finish reading a story called *Bungalow Bill*. Ms. M couldn't refuse, and the continuing story of Bungalow Bill burst into life, just like *The Escapades of Mr. Kite*! All the attentive students cheered, and our departure was postponed, watching them be captivated by another fun-filled fable. After the last sentence was read, we expressed our thanks for sharing their time with us, and suddenly, their expressions changed to disappointment. We exchanged our sad farewells, and the second we walked outside, our following Abelets darted off the playground to reunite with us. Fantebela and Ulap grabbed my hands, and all of us headed to who-knows-where.

Chapter Six

Getting Better

AS WE TRAVELED ON, I ASKED ULAP and Fantebela if there was a chance of seeing Hojn, Ginor, and Roggee again. Although there was no response, I was optimistic it eventually would happen. For some unknown reason, there had been a curious connection between us, and I was hoping to see them again. Those thoughts were interrupted after coming across the most exquisite violet flowers bordering both sides of a concrete stairway. Our downhill climb begun, and being cautious didn't prevent me from almost taking yet another tumble. My friends grabbed my hands, and, after reaching the bottom, I saw a jumbo sign in the distance, which read, "Welcome to Pepperland!" I jokingly asked if we would start sneezing when we arrived. After the giggling quieted down, Ulap declared, "It won't be long before we reach our next destination." The word "destination" sent chills up and down my spine, and I didn't know whether to be excited or scared. He observed the look on my face and said to me, "Stop worrying!" Everything was only getting better, so I decided to just let it be. Maybe the only thing I should be worried about was waking up.

Assorted shades of pink flowers loomed high above the long and winding road we were traveling. As we walked on, those thoughts of Hojn, Ginor, and Roggee immediately flooded back. In some puzzling way, there had been that unusual kind of bond, and my nosiness had finally reached its peak. Therefore, I gathered the strength to ask Fantebela once more if we would see them in the sometime in the future. To my astonishment, she finally answered, "I'm sure those three are probably off somewhere, getting into some kind of monkey business. And, if you ask me, most likely way too much monkey business!" Although her response caught me off guard, my instincts told me those three charismatic faces would reappear before my eyes yet again!

The sun's rays glistened upon our arrival in the land of Pepper. We climbed a trail that reached the peak of a hill and proceeded our downhill climb to the other side. A waterfall showered warm water over us, and the welcoming drops felt just like September in the rain. We cautiously maneuvered our way down the moss-covered rocks, where I almost slipped. Thankfully, I was able to grasp Fantebela's and Ulap's outstretched hands. After our feet touched the ground, my instincts confirmed we had reached that so-called destination. Before I could take another breath, a monstrous yellow submarine began surfacing in their vast ocean. My body stiffened, realizing that big hunk of steel was eagerly waiting for us. Fantebela also stiffened her body, trying her best to imitate me. Ulap realized she was teasing me and stated, "Honey don't do that!" Her playful face looked at me as if she had the devil in her heart, yet I already knew she was an angel by my side. Ulap turned and whispered to me, "You should know by now she loves you."

I was flabbergasted by his comment, but it was my remark that was so much more shocking. "And I love her too!"

Our following Abelets would not be joining us on the sub, but it was understood we would be reunited following our underwater excursion. As Fantebela, Ulap, and I advanced ahead, we were stopped dead in our tracks after hearing some loud, rustling sounds. After glancing around, we spotted some familiar faces trying their best to hide behind some bushes. Rather than looking like three cool cats, Roggee, Hojn, and Ginor were jumping up and down, looking more like three cool monkeys. They smugly announced, "Sorry we're late, but we were having breakfast with the sheik of Araby in the palace of the king of the birds!" They knew that none of us believed their far-fetched tale by our unconvincing faces, but their reappearance lifted my spirits to new heights. However, that uplifting feeling quickly diminished the second I thought the inside of the sub may feel like a matchbox. Amid some trepidation, yet with loads of anticipation, we made our way to a tiny boat waiting to transport us to the yellow monstrosity.

Chapter Seven

Magical Mystery Tour

THE BOAT SHOWED NO MERCY, ROCKING BACK and forth, transporting us to the yellow submarine in Pepperland. I sensed my color may have turned green; however, nothing could have interfered with our upcoming voyage. As soon as the two vessels united, we scrambled up some ironclad steps secured on the side of the massive sub. Once reaching the top deck, we encountered more stairs leading us straight into the belly of the monster. The steps were steep and narrow, and my friends no longer could hold my hands to help me. Ulap had already reached the bottom and was waiting for me when I almost tripped. He screeched, "Grab on to the railing!" In spite of all the danger, if I fell, I knew he would immediately catch me and hold me tight. The moment I touched the last step, the laughter erupted when Ulap announced that I had just earned the new title of their Day Tripper! Within seconds, the sound of the engine intensified, and the mammoth machine began to submerge deeper into the depths of what was to become a new world.

We chugged along at a snail's pace while I remained awestruck, gazing out my crystal-clear window. It was unlike the other ones that were dreadfully cloudy, and I surmised they wiped it spotless for me not to miss a solitary thing. Not a second was wasted while I soaked it all in like a dry sponge. The effervescent coral reefs were as brilliant as the dazzling rainbow fish. Nearby were turtles, sea horses, jellyfish, and other living beings swimming in an array of astonishing colors. And to no great revelation, each had an extra eye. Every so often, one would sneak a peek through my window where my nose remained pressed against the pane. Whether a dream or a reality, that'll be the day any of this could ever be erased from my memory.

The amazing life under water kept me entranced until Fantebela broke my spell and whispered, "Do you want to know a secret?" There was no time to answer before she whispered even lower. "We are drifting in the Sour Milk Sea with the sea of monsters, and I am the walrus." She made a funny face, and it immediately dawned on me that she was behaving beyond silly. Not a second passed before we burst into so much laughter that we could hardly breathe.

Hojn glanced my way, and in an overly dramatic voice, stated, "Oh! Darling, it pleases us to see you so happy."

Without any hesitation, I responded, "Please please me anytime you'd like!" Their sense of humor was always welcomed, and mine was returning after my little friends snatched me, or should I say rescued me?

Our underwater expedition cruised along, but my mood shifted to a somber tone when Ulap began educating me of how the bottom of the ocean was filled with Pepperland Laid waste. He continued to inform me the sea of holes in the bottom of the water generates life from the laid waste, which, in turn, creates an everlasting sea of time. My full attention of how the life cycle occurs abruptly ended the instant I saw her. My heart began to pound as she swam out of her glorious garden. She was a true vision of loveliness while maneuvering her way toward a heart-shaped log. Roggee clearly explained, "After Rita emerges, she rests on her most treasured Norwegian Wood and spreads her love of the loved to all creatures." Within minutes, she gracefully danced by my window, and electricity raced through my body when our eyes met. At the same moment, I could feel her kindness plunging into the depths of my soul. She was hoping I could come into her garden, and at the same time, I was wishing she could come into the sub. Realizing neither option was possible, an overwhelming sense of sadness rushed over me. Thousands of bubbles surrounded my window, and there was no question that it was lovely Rita blowing kisses as we drifted away.

My affectionate thoughts of Rita were thankfully interrupted when a lone beluga whale swam by. Shadowing behind him were sharks, manatees, and dolphins. One by one, they nudged their way to my window, and our noses touched as if no glass separated us. I was overcome with emotion while observing the magical world before my eyes. Ulap softly spoke, "What you're doing is feeling and embracing the pure beauty within *your* soul." It led me wondering, *What would it be like if everyone took a good look to feel and embrace the pure beauty within their soul?*

The roaring noise of the sub was gradually winding down, and everyone was aware that we would be rising to the surface at any moment. We made our way to the stairs where my mini sidekicks assumed I'd be taking another tumble. All eyes were on me, and I do mean all eyes. Since my tripping had become part of my regular routine, they thought it best for me to walk up the steps in front of them in case I may trip and fall backwards. They were treating me as if *I* were a baby, but I thought, perhaps was it more like everybody's trying to be *my* baby? Whatever the reason, one thing was for darn sure, our Magical Mystery Tour was surely magical! I was confident I must be dreaming, but if that were true, then tell me why there was no convincing me. Regrettably, our underwater voyage had reached its end.

Chapter Eight

Here Comes the Sun!

ALL OF US ASSEMBLED INTO THE SAME small boat that transported us to the sub and headed back to the land of Pepper. All the Abelets were expecting us, and after disembarking, I waved to them like any well-known celebrity. Although I noticed more had disappeared, our hike continued with the scenery showing off in its typical fashion. Another imposing waterfall appeared, and high above on a hill, I caught a glimpse of a lady transfixed in all the endless views. When I questioned Fantebela about her, she nonchalantly answered, "Oh, that's just the fool on the hill. She's a woman who everyone loves to tease, but she's anything but a fool." The lady instantly spotted us and started her lengthy climb down. Her strawberry-blonde hair flowed wildly down to her waist, and her ruby-red lips highlighted her large white teeth.

She flaunted a playful grin and declared, "Hi, I'm Dizzy Miss Lizzy!" It was obvious how teasing made sense with that offbeat name of hers. Her demeanor was uplifting, and she asked if she could keep us company. Of course, both Fantebela and I were more than delighted to have her join us.

The three of us soon caught up with Ulap, Hojn, Roggee and Ginor, but our lagging Abelets had fallen way behind. I sensed Ulap becoming flustered by them not keeping up the pace with the rest of us. He elected to be stern, which wasn't an easy task, yet he had no problem in achieving that challenge. He reached into his checkered pants for his dependable whistle, and with a deep breath, vigorously blew into it. My ears and everyone else's rang for at least five blooming minutes! In a flash, the Abelets sprinted at lightning speed and caught up with us. They called Ulap a meanie for blowing his whistle, and Ulap responded by also calling them Meanies for trailing so far behind. At that moment, it was unanimously agreed that in everyone's honor, our future parading would be known as The March of the Meanies. Of course, we all had a good laugh at our humorous new parade name. It never ceased to amaze me how their quirky sense of humor consistently placed smiles on their faces, including mine. I elected to add Meanies to my vocabulary, and then decided, why not Peeps too!

The mighty sun that was hiding behind their majestic mountains eventually chose to peek out. With loads of enthusiasm, all the Meanies roared, "Here comes the sun!" The exhilaration of watching the Sun King rise caused me to question the name of their mystifying planet.

Ginor, who was standing by my side, became my target for asking about the name of this heavenly place. He performed a soft-shoe shuffle while proudly beaming, "Why, it's the one and only Savoy Truffle!"

I wittingly replied, "You sure do a great shuffle on Truffle!" We giggled, but once I thought about the name Truffle, it reminded me of a delicious piece of chocolate from home. I imagined I'd soon be waking up there, but then I thought, *Please…not yet.*

Fantebela, Ms. Lizzy, and I slowed down our pace, believing it had become *our* turn to fall way behind everyone. Our unending chitchat made our moments together exceptionally special. Ms. Lizzy was referring to Fantebela when she questioned me, "Ain't she sweet?"

I teasingly responded, "Not as sweet as you!"

Fantebela formed a funny face and repeatedly asked, "Do you love me do you?"

Without hesitation, I responded, "If I say yes, will you let me stay here forever?"

She answered, "Only if you can shrink and make funny faces!" Never knowing what would be spouting out of her mouth produced more laughter, and with another girl by our side, that laughter only grew louder. Tons of kidding around was a major part of their existence, but it was their real love that endlessly flowed. It was such an honor to be such a friend in their mesmerizing land of Truffle.

Chapter Nine

I'll Follow the Sun

AS WE TREKKED ON, AN OLD-FASHIONED BARN dominated the stunning landscape in the distance. Upon our arrival, cows, sheep, goats, pigs, ducks, and chickens were roaming freely, but not a single soul was around. After peeking inside the barn, I was relieved after witnessing several Peeps tending to the four- and two-legged creatures. We exchanged friendly waves, and immediately, I realized we were just passing through. We continued to walk for what seemed like miles, and I was feeling grateful for my newfound candy-striped sneakers mysteriously surfacing on my big feet. As our hike commenced, it suddenly came to a halt. We all stood motionless, not only staring at a fork in the road but also at one another. Ulap insisted I choose which path we should follow. Since stepping off the spaceship, he led the way as our leader, and for some reason, he wanted me to assume responsibility by taking charge. I guess he needed me to carry that weight he had been carrying throughout our journey. Without hesitation, I chose the path where the sun rays glistened through the treetops and announced, "I'll follow the sun." Despite the fluttering butterflies in my stomach, I accepted my new role like a genuine sergeant. With my little friends trailing behind me, we proceeded parading down the sun-drenched path. After hiking for some time, I led them down Cayenne Bluff's Trail, and that's when my ears perked up, hearing some giggling sounds. I quickly learned they were giggling at me, and within seconds, I joined them. Carrying that weight must have carried me away! At that moment, I understood how they loved to tease, but I also understood there was no such thing as I me mine on their planet. Fantebela raced over and embraced me. I lovingly said, "Where have you been all my life?" She simply pointed to my heart.

Chapter Ten

A Taste of Honey

WE EVENTUALLY REACHED A MEADOW WHERE THE heather filled the air with a sweet-smelling aroma. The sun generated an enormous amount of warmth, and in no time, the Peeps opened a quilt bursting with an array of vibrant colors. The grass seemed rather damp, and Ulap suggested we search for another location to lay it down. After some deliberating, he suggested, "Why don't we do it in the road where it's as dry as a bone?" After inspecting the heavily padded quilt, we all agreed it would be suitable to place it on the grass. All the Peeps assisted and were careful not to squish any of the delicate flowers. How they concealed the multicolored quilt, along with a variety of baskets that sprang up from nowhere, was just another mystery. The redheaded Eleanor Rigby took charge, and a scrumptious picnic sprang to life. Apples, blueberries, cherries, watermelons, oranges, grapes, blackberries, and heaps of others spilled over on the quilt. The time had come to indulge our hungry bellies. Our mouths began watering at the sight of all the luscious treats at our fingertips. My taste buds were instantly awakened by a taste of honey before treating myself to the other goodies. Every bite was as delicious as the Fudgareli ice cream I devoured not long ago. Again, I asked how it was possible everything could taste so delicious if I were only dreaming.

Glancing around, I observed a variety of butterflies, ladybugs, grasshoppers, praying mantis, and many others mingling together. There were squirrels, chipmunks and rabbits mischievously romping around, playing what we call hide-'n'-seek back home. From time to time, the fuzzy critters would visit us, and we would graciously share our treats. The sparrows, cardinals, blue jays, woodpeckers, hummingbirds, and dozens more would occasionally land on our laps and shoulders. High above soared a lone blackbird, who I suspected was the great protector of the entire flock. Before long, a fine-looking parakeet landed on Hojn's shoulder as if they were long lost buddies. The bird began singing a soothing tune, and Hojn joined him. Their interaction was spellbinding, and I expressed to my friend, "You and your bird can sing like angels." Both winked with their third eye, which triggered an instant melting of my heart. The parakeet soon opted to settle on my shoulder, singing the same tune. The second I tried joining my feathered friend, his wings began to flutter and off he flew.

Hojn chuckled and remarked, "Maybe you should just stick to talking!"

Nearby were beavers, ducks, geese, swans, frogs, and many others playing together in their sun-drenched pond. Out in the fields, ponies were playing, and there's not a soul in either one of our worlds who doesn't dig a pony! Roggee was frolicking among the gentle creatures, looking just like Mother Nature's son. There were dogs, puppies, cats, and kittens also playing, but to my dismay, a lone dog sat all by himself until Fantebela cried out, "Hey Bulldog, come here!" Like lightning, he ran over, plopped himself on her lap, and began slobbering all over her. It reminded me of all the slobbering in *The Escapades of Mr. Kite*. We watched her wipe herself with tons and tons of napkins that each of us handed her. Soon an adorable kitten named Baby purred her way over, and without a second to spare,

Bulldog jumped off Fantebela's lap and ran to her. With his waterlogged tongue still hanging, he slobbered all over Baby. The rest of us could hear Fantebela yell, "Please, Bull, leave my kitten alone!" He then sprinted back to Fantebela's lap with his tongue still dangling, and that's when we heard her whisper to him, "I'm counting on you to take good care of my Baby after I leave, so please don't let me down." Bull shook his head and then leaped off her lap onto mine. It had become my turn to be handed tons and tons of napkins.

Not a moment passed without being captivated by the furry and nonfurry creatures interacting with one another. Ginor caught me off guard when he asked, "Aren't you curious about how many little friends are scurrying about?" That thought never crossed my mind, and it certainly was an odd question.

He showed such disappointment after I responded, "Not really." But when my curiosity finally caught up with me, I began counting one and one is two and on and on and on. It seemed like hours before I proudly and smugly answered, "909!"

He apologetically responded, "Sorry, but it's one *after* 909!"

Such a bizarre way of replying, but it didn't even compare to our child of nature returning from the fields, singing, "Everybody's got something to hide except me and my monkey!" The rest of us were downright speechless listening to Roggee sing his wacky jingle. All of us shook our heads for no one grasped his sense of humor at first. Of course, it only took seconds for us to realize his usual teasing ways. He loved being in the spotlight and chose to share it with the friendly monkey jumping up and down on his back. The shy one was enjoying a good time spoofing all of us, and his contagious laughter quickly spread to everyone.

Despite the fact our fun-filled picnic had reached its end, everyone remained in good spirits. Ginor, with his uncanny sense of wit, announced, "Time to go; time for the next show!"

Jokingly, I responded, "Look at you with a little rhyme after mealtime!" After our giggling, we began packing up the baskets and the quilt. But right before we were ready to scurry off to our next adventure, I turned to my friends and broadcasted, "Please don't ever change." Yes, they were tiny. And yes, they were giants.

Chapter Eleven

All You Need Is Love

MY CANDY-STRIPED SNEAKERS WERE NOT ON MY big feet when my little friends appeared at my bedside, yet with all our hiking, they turned into genuine lifesavers. It was as though they miraculously attached themselves to my feet, like the ruby slippers in *The Wizard of Oz*. Not only had they materialized, but my pajamas changed into vibrant colorful clothing. Although my pinching had long ended, my thoughts persisted when unexpectedly a most preposterous one popped into my head. I visualized my mother attempting to chase the mysterious strangers away while frantically shrieking, "You better keep your hands off my baby!" But the irony of all ironies, it's been those very same hands that have been with me every step of the way.

My motherly visions were left behind the second we entered an underground cave. Within minutes, we maneuvered our way, leading us to a catwalk with guardrails protecting us from the rippling stream below. Brilliant shades of blue glowed over and under a bridge leading us into a secret cavern. After walking a few more steps, we approached boundless levels of wooden stairs where I was afforded the opportunity to hold my friends' hands again. With my comrades by my side, there was no apprehension in our downward climb into another part of their private world. The instant my feet touched the bottom of their secluded sanctuary, it was a divine celestial encounter. My anticipation rose to new heights after we gathered on a stone floor, which was unpredictably comfortable. Massive walls displayed endless inspirational quotes and chills joined my goose bumps after reading the first quote by an unknown author. Mutual feelings between my hand-holding friends and me were affectionately expressed. I took a deep breath to digest every word. "When you really love someone, age, distance, height, weight is only a number." More heartfelt emotions were shared when reading more powerful words on their walls. Quote after quote held me captive, causing me to feel hypnotized and mesmerized at the same time. My thoughts rushed back to when those crashing sounds of thunder awakened me. I believed my troubled world had turned upside down, but then some strange creatures showed up and turned it right-side up.

With a Little Help from My Friends

Perhaps, if we all had an extra eye, kindness and love could triumph, creating a true brotherhood of man. My wish was to prolong our stay in their spiritual haven, but I knew our next venture was waiting. Before departing, Ulap proclaimed, "*You* can't buy love, and *you* can't buy *me* love, but if you have love and give love, you have everything." Ulap was right; all you need is love.

Chapter Twelve

Act Naturally

AFTER EXITING THEIR ENCHANTED CAVE, WE MARCHED back to the picnic grounds where all the delightful creatures were catching an afternoon siesta. They appeared to be in a deep sleep, yet after hearing some unusual noises, the stillness was suddenly interrupted. We were listening to what sounded like babies crying, and that's when we saw several stray piggies appearing lost. Ginor instinctively raced over and ran in circles for what seemed like hours, gathering them in his arms. His face beamed with pride the second he reunited them to their most relieved mother. The kind and thoughtful Ginor was instantly nicknamed our "Piggy Hero." Remarkably, my feet had grown weary just watching him scramble all over on his rescue mission. Roggee, being his clown self, also looked exhausted and babbled, "I'm too tired to walk anymore, so I think I'll just drive my car!" Knowing there are no cars on Truffle, the rest of us burst into laughter. Again, we rose to the occasion to be his loyal audience when his unpredictable humor would catch us by surprise.

Our piggy episode had ended, and our hike set off at a leisurely stride. Shortly after, Fantebela and I deliberately fell behind Ms. Lizzy and the rest of the Peeps. I silently thought how fear had become a thing of the past, anticipation had become a thing of the present, and the unknown remained a thing of the future. I forgot to remember to forget my fears since it had become such a joy to act naturally. Fantebela, who had been repeatedly calling my name, ultimately caught my attention. I apologized for being in a trance, to which she lovingly responded, "That's all right, I understand." But did she? Could she have known what I was thinking?

I turned to her and sighed. "No matter where you go, I'll be on my way to be right beside you." She tenderly reached for my hand and simply smiled.

Chapter Thirteen

Nothin' Shakin'

FANTEBELA AND I TRAIPSED ACROSS THE PICNIC grounds, trying our best to catch up with everyone. We headed down a mountainous trail and into the thick brush where they were patiently waiting for us. Not only were they waiting, but hundreds of animals were also anticipating our arrival. However, those animals were not of the same kind as the ones we shared our picnic with. Directly in front of our faces stood the wildest of beasts. As we drew closer, my eyes clearly saw them, and their noses clearly smelled us. Their three eyes were of no surprise, but them roaming around freely certainly was. Back on Earth, they would be deemed ferocious, but then again, we were not back on Earth. Was it conceivable that dangerous animals would be inhabiting their peaceful planet? And was it also possible the peace-loving times on Truffle were ending? Fear that had long faded rapidly returned, gaining momentum like an out-of-control wildfire. The lions, tigers, cougars, zebras, rhinos, elephants, cheetahs, giraffes, gorillas, panthers, bears, and scores of others were seemingly looking forward to their next prey. My deserted pinching had leaped into action, but there would be no waking up. I tried convincing myself the Peeps must be carrying weapons to protect us from the terrifying creatures. Just when I expected Ulap may give the order to shoot, he asked me to look up to the sky. The most spectacular rainbow appeared, and somewhere over that rainbow, a heavenly intervention took place. Without any explanation, a calmness swept over me, and the terror steadily withdrew from my trembling body. Ulap watched me as the so-called savage beasts headed their way toward us, but he already knew there'd be nothin' shakin' on me. In some mystifying way, all of us were spiritually connected. I knew, from that day forward, I'd be watching rainbows forevermore.

The once-frayed fibers of my nerves no longer existed, but the time had arrived for me to confess that I assumed the Peeps were concealing some weapons to protect us. Ulap looked straight at me and calmly said, "On our planet, we have no ferocious creatures, and we have no deadly weapons, especially guns. And, if we did, we want you to understand that our happiness is a warm gun that shoots only love." Such a perplexing statement, but unmistakably, his words were fully understood. In the meantime, all the four-legged creatures were congregating around me, craving my attention. A tiger wasted no time nudging me, and we played together before many of the others joined us. A few lions attempted to lure me into their den until Ulap interjected and made it clear that under no circumstance could they keep me. As I turned around, Mr. Grizzly Bear was stomping his way over to give me a great, big grizzly hug. I tried remaining composed, but the thought of him squishing me to pieces caused me to somewhat panic. Ms. Lizzy jumped to my rescue and hollered to Mr. Grizzly not to be a bad boy and squeeze me too tight. While making his way over, he let out a chilling growl and then embraced me as gently as a pussy cat. Once again, I was reassured no living soul on Truffle could be bad to anyone on their planet or be bad to me.

After many hours of playtime, I plopped on the grass next to Fantebela before a new round of interaction would begin with my new playmates. It was short-lived as soon as Mimjie, the jumbo elephant, stomped her way over. She effortlessly picked us up with her trunk, and our tour of the grounds was set in motion. We clung on like professionals while viewing their picturesque terrain against their sapphire sky. The friendly monkeys and harmonious birds were the happiest of creatures as we paraded by. Upon returning, our giant friend bowed her head, and we slid down her trunk, like little children whizzing down a slide. Both of us presented her with a big kiss and then darted off to join the others who were eagerly waiting.

    We resumed our playtime with all the animals until noticing Ulap reach for his trusty whistle. To our delight, he had a change of heart and returned it to his pocket. However, it wasn't much longer when he motioned that everyone needed to say our goodbyes. We were having the time of our lives, so how come we had to leave? There would be no answer, yet I longed to run to those so-called wild beasts for one last hug, but that earsplitting whistle of Ulap's changed my mind. We waved farewell, and then we were off and running to our next exploration.

Chapter Fourteen

Baby's in Black

MORE PEEPS VANISHED, AND I WONDERED IF we would be re-united just like we had been with my three monkeys, Hojn, Roggee, and Ginor! My wondering ended when we approached a grassy hill ready to be climbed. We navigated our way up while holding hands and, as usual, I almost took another tumble. When reaching the peak, we shared a bird's-eye view of a ball field below and saw many new faces peering up at us. After scaling our way down, they greeted us with the expectation of joining them in a ball game. The field looked like a carbon copy from back home, except for their oversize colored ball that stood out like a gigantic sore thumb! I suspected they may have spied on Earth to duplicate our ball games. My suspicions were sidetracked when hearing Fantebela holler to Ulap, "If we're going to play ball, you better take out some insurance on me baby!" Everyone chuckled, knowing that gigantic ball couldn't hurt a fly. More grumbling words sprouted from her sassy mouth directed straight at Ulap. "And I want you on the same team with me!" He tried rationalizing with her that it would be up to the captains who would make the final decisions. She created another funny face, paying no attention to him, and whether it would be sooner or later, we believed we needed to prepare ourselves for more of Fantebela's antics.

Our trailing Peeps chose to sit on the sidelines and become rooting fans for both teams. Meanwhile, Captain Nitmar chose me on *The Gray's* with Ulap and Hojn. As anticipated, Fantebela wasted no time causing quite the raucous for not being on the same team with Ulap. She was chosen with Roggee and Ginor on the Blacks by Captain Keder. Her protesting words to the captains were clearly and loudly heard. Ulap was rather embarrassed and spoke to Fantebela, "Honey, you can't do that!" We were speechless while expecting at any moment the true battle was soon to erupt. But suddenly, a mischievous expression crept up on her face, which stunned us all. Everyone was dumbfounded when she declared she had been teasing us the entire time. We were even more shocked when Ulap announced, "I knew you were!"

She playfully replied, "I knew that you knew!"

He cleverly responded, "I knew that you knew that I knew!" All of us were trying to follow their whacky banter, and our heads were going back and forth like we were at a ping-pong match. The two pranksters were unrelenting, and their so-called teasing exploded into a comical revolution 1 to a sidesplitting revolution 9. We were honestly enjoying their unconventional comedy antics when Ulap finally surrendered. He good-humoredly stated that it was time to move on to the real revolution between The Blacks and The Grays! Color shirts were handed out, and everyone put them on with ease with one exception! Finally, I stretched mine to the max and awkwardly tugged it over my head, and that's when we all heard, "Let's play ball!"

I sprinted to left field, giggling how that position suited me perfectly. Not far behind me was Ulap, scrambling to centerfield while shouting how humorous it was that he's in Gray and his baby's in black. As soon as he spoke those words, Fantebela, that funny-faced baby of his, stepped up to the plate and belted a fly ball that zoomed directly toward me. With boundless confidence, I shouted, "You don't have a chance, my little friend; you'll be mine in a second!" The oversized ball whizzed straight at me and smoothly landed in my hands. My team wildly cheered, but to my sheer horror, it silently rolled out of my hands in agonizing slow motion. Those thunderous cheers were immediately followed by a ghastly silence. Luckily, Ulap came to my rescue and scooped up the ball and threw it to second base while my blushing face was trying to reclaim its natural color. Meanwhile, Fantebela ran as fast as her tiny legs could carry her and was tagged out by a Peep named Cire. The only voice we heard echoing from the outfield was none other than Ulap's.

He good-naturedly bellowed, "I got a woman out!" Fantebela concocted another one of her funny faces while I was hoping my natural color would come back to mine. When my final "at bat" arrived, the score was tied at 2–2. And like a much-loved hero, I miraculously hit the winning homerun and felt completely exonerated! After the game ended, we parked ourselves on the grass to recap the fun-filled moments we shared. Although we didn't hear Ulap's announcement it was time to go, we surely heard that earsplitting whistle of his! We parted ways with our good-natured teammates and then darted off to our next caper.

Chapter Fifteen

Ticket to Ride

WE JOURNEYED OUR WAY BACK TO THE open picnic grounds once again. Within seconds, everyone tilted their heads toward the sky, and I wasted no time joining them in their riveted state. My mouth dropped opened once I saw a magnificent hot-air balloon traveling toward us. After it touched the ground, I could barely see a shadowy figure strutting down the steps. However, as he advanced toward us, his visible ruggedness couldn't go unnoticed. His chestnut-brown hair was combed back to perfection, exposing the biggest nose of all the Peeps. He saluted us with a giant grin and broadcasted, "Mean Mr. Mustard at your service." I stood erect while barely breathing and saluted him alongside everyone. All of us maintained a stiff-like position and finally exhaled a huge sigh of relief after hearing "At ease!" Unquestionably, he was as much respected as he was admired.

Carolyn Addie

    The so-called mean man was also known as "The Captain," and we all intently listened as he straightaway explained there would be good news as well as bad. The good news came first. We were informed a few of us would be soaring on a scenic ride, and the bad news...there was only room for four of us. With a commanding voice, he continued, "Four Golden Tickets are in the offering for a trip of a lifetime!"
    Without hesitation, Ulap leaned over and whispered in my ear, "I'll get you to choose who will be the lucky ones." I was stunned at his request and thought, *How could he ask me who should go and who should stay?* Not another word was muttered in my no-win situation.
    Thank goodness Ginor noted my dilemma and stated, "I have better things to do, so don't bother me." His answer was baffling at first, but it became quite evident that he would relinquish his seat as an act of kindness. Nevertheless, Ginor's thoughtfulness did not solve my difficult predicament. Of course, *I* would be going and understood Ulap would be by my side, but who else? I shuffled their names in my head and knew there was no way I could leave my funny-faced sidekick behind. Therefore, my awkward choice dwindled right down to Hojn and Roggee. Luckily, I was rescued by Ms. Lizzy and her buddies, Tepe and Liavio. They suggested for them to play in a game known as "The Crazy Crying Shadow Contest." It was played from time to time when challenging predicaments needed a decision,

and this was one of those times. Ms. Lizzy explained that when the sun peeks out from behind The Crying Tree, the contestants shed their tears, which mysteriously causes their shadow to grow taller and taller. Ms. Lizzy continued to enlighten me that whoever produces the tallest shadow wins the contest and the ticket to ride in the balloon.

Before I knew what happened, the overly excited Peeps hollered to Hojn and Roggee, "Get ready to cry for a shadow!" I was baffled by the craziness of it all and believed it had to be the most harebrained competition ever invented. If a dream it would win first prize, and if not a dream, it would still win first prize!

Hojn and Roggee lined up when I hesitantly but willingly accepted their ludicrous way of playing such an outlandish game. The almighty sun was preparing to peek out, and once in perfect position, the words flowed from Ms. Lizzy's mouth. "Let the battle begin!" In a flash, it turned into a crazy mad-cap scene.

Waterworks cascaded down their cheeks as the Peeps continued to roar, "Cry baby cry!" Within a matter of minutes, Hojn shed more tears, creating the tallest shadow and was declared the victor. Despite the fact Roggee lost the most preposterous contest ever invented, he couldn't have been happier for me. Regrettably, I was not feeling the same happiness.

My heart melted when he said, "Hope you enjoy the ride, and when it's over, I'll be right here waiting for you." I slowly mounted the stairs with Ulap, Fantebela, Hojn, and The Captain. As the balloon floated upward, I covered my face, concealing my tears.

Trying to hide my emotions, I leaned over the side and hollered out to Roggee, "I'll be back!"

Chapter Sixteen

It's Only Love

NO AMOUNT OF MONEY COULD EVER PERSUADE ME to fly, but I understood there was no other option. However, once viewing their heart-stopping sites, my phobia of flying instantly evaporated. Anytime at all you think nothing can get better, it should be time for you to think again! The beauty of their stunning scenery melted every ounce of my fear. The Captain insisted we seize every moment while handing us a pair of three-eyed goggles. We dutifully placed them on, and I apologized for not having an extra eye. All of them wasted no time convincing me that to them, it couldn't be more visible.

We drifted over the sparkling waters, and I had high hopes of capturing a glimpse of the Octopus's Garden to see my friend, Rita. She was nowhere in sight, but my disappointment subsided once everybody started singing, "My Bonnie lies over the ocean." I instinctively jumped in, and after the last note, I questioned Ulap how he knew my planet's song. He replied with a huge grin that he wrote it! Although his answer was rather amusing, nothing could distract me from the spellbinding views. The breeze whipped around and suddenly blew Hojn's hair over his eyes.

With a stone-cold face, he asked me, "Can you lend me your comb?"

I replied with a sheepish grin, "Sorry, but I didn't have time to pack one!" Everyone chuckled except for Mr. Mustard, but he soon joined in with the rest of us. We were aware how he cherished being The Captain of his balloon, and we also knew that underneath his four-foot frame stood a gentle giant.

As we glided along, our Captain asked if anyone would like to experience a once-in-a-lifetime ride on the edge of the balloon. Predictably, the daring Fantebela chimed in and eagerly volunteered. He carefully hooked her up with a special safety harness, and off she flew. Periodically, she would wave to us, and I marveled at her fearlessness. For a moment, I was tempted to try; however, I dismissed it in much less time. I watched her as she swayed back and forth, but when the wind picked up, it brought the ride to its finale. Captain Mustard understood the necessary precaution to haul my little friend back in and asked her, "Do you know what to do?" She nodded her head and obediently tightened the harness around her.

He hoisted her back into the balloon, and after Fantebela recaptured her breath, she impishly said to me, "Now, it's your turn!"

Whether or not I was dreaming, I politely responded, "Maybe later." We both laughed, knowing there was no chance of that materializing. Mr. Mustard piped in and said if the wind died down and I had a change of heart, he would take good care of me. I declined his offer but was elated, keeping him company as he navigated his most beloved balloon.

A cool breeze streamed through the air, gently caressing our faces. It happened to be a true paradise without a single worry or care in the world. If you've got trouble, this was where you wanted to be. If I were returning home, I'd be searchin' a lifetime for a place just like this. It simply could be defined with three little words, it's only love. Sadly, our sightseeing tour was approaching its end. We headed back to the picnic grounds, and after our smooth landing, the time had come to bid goodbye to our Captain. A crushing sense of sorrow entered my heart, believing I would never see him again. We were bidding our goodbyes when he fondly winked at me. Next he brought his hand to his forehead, and with much gratitude, I returned his salute. He then clicked his heels, did an about-face, and departed into his prized balloon. And just like magic, he disappeared into the sky. Once seeing Roggee, we both smiled, then ran to one another and embraced. Soon after, everyone assembled, and as usual, we set off to our next escapade.

Chapter Seventeen

Baby It's You

AS OUR NEWEST TREK WAS UNDERWAY, THE landscape quickly transformed into blazing shades of reds and oranges. Prior to hiking any further, we stopped to witness the day approaching its end. All of us watched the glorious sun gradually begin its descent behind the snowcapped mountains. Oddly, their sun was setting in the north as opposed to setting in the west on Earth. My friends enlightened me that they look to the north to capture the rays as the day begins to fade into darkness. They all sing a special tribute to the sun and express their appreciation with only a northern song. Not knowing the words, I asked if I could hum along with them. At once, Fantebela's funny face cropped up to remind me of Hojn's sentiments when his parakeet landed on my shoulder. She playfully repeated his comment, "Maybe you should just stick to talking!"

Lam and Slauk were the last two Peeps who hadn't vanished and were still trailing behind us. Surprisingly, both threw their hands up and waved farewell to the rest of us. The reason they chose to leave in that manner, as opposed to simply disappearing like the others, was somewhat perplexing. Nevertheless, the rest of us continued walking when Ulap announced, "After we pass Moonlight Bay, we will have reached our next destination." Oh, that daunting "destination" word again! Chills returned just like they had once before, but this time, no fear, only anticipation.

We picked up our stride when Fantebela unexpectedly came to an abrupt standstill. She appeared to be in a spellbinding trance, staring into the sky. She turned my way and passionately questioned, "Do you see those millions and millions of twinkling stars?" There was no time to answer before she pointed to the one that shined like a sparkling diamond. Her voice resumed with passion, "She's my favorite, and I named her Lucy."

Curiously, I asked, "Since she sparkles like a diamond, why aren't you calling her Lucy in the sky with diamonds?" She was overcome with emotion at my suggestion, and her face began to sparkle…just like Lucy's.

With a Little Help from My Friends

    We reached the inlet where the moon's reflection shimmered on the bay. Apparently, our destination was drawing closer, and after a few more steps, it was as though someone turned on a light switch. The luminous beams surrounded a white castle-like building appearing as though it were daytime. We strolled up the steps where a welcome sign was secured on the door, but we never had the chance to open it. Like lightning, hundreds upon hundreds of Peeps on the other side swung it wide open. All the ones who had vanished during our travels resurfaced together with countless new faces. They sprang from everywhere, shouting, "Surprise! Surprise!" I turned my head to see who they were surprising, and that's when I heard their thunderous voices explode, "Baby it's you!" Before I could even blink, everyone was singing "Happy Birthday" to me.

Chapter Eighteen

Come Together

AFTER ENTERING THE HALL, I RECOGNIZED THE Peeps who had disappeared throughout our travels and so many new faces. They had all come together for the liveliest of welcomes, and my spirits were lifted higher than Mr. Mustard's hot-air balloon! The hall was a carnival of light-spewing electricity throughout the room. Multicolored balloons towered above, creating a most-festive atmosphere. A regal chair resembling a queen's throne sprang into view, and I surmised it was there especially for me. Ulap and Fantebela clutched my hands and lovingly escorted me to the majestic chair. Both held on to me while I prayed my unsteady legs wouldn't give way. They assisted in helping me into the seat while at the same time passionately broadcasting, "Her Majesty has arrived!"

    The energized crowd greeted me as the excitement continued to escalate. The new faces, as well as the ones who had been trailing behind us, were chanting my name. I tried to overpower their voices by hollering to all the newfound Peeps, "You know my name, but I don't know any of yours!" At the same time, I was thrilled recognizing all the ones who disappeared throughout our adventures. I couldn't contain myself as I began shouting, "I remember you and you and you!" Enthusiasm continued to soar while we greeted each other, and I secretly wondered if they could hear the thumping of my heart.

    That excitement ended when Ulap interrupted the greetings and strutted to the center of the hall. Everything came to a standstill, and a curious silence surfaced as the Peeps scrambled to the sidelines. My friend cleared his throat, and in a soft voice, explained how crucial it was for them to bring me into *their* world. He expressed how they needed to rescue me from *my* world, which had been crushing my spirits. The hushed room listened as his words further echoed, "We need your disheartened mood to be lifted, knowing you are a loving and kind soul. Not long ago, we visited your planet where peace and love once existed. We believe you can bring that love and peace home with you for the commonwealth of all mankind. We have unwavering faith your spirit can and will be restored, therefore, on your special day, embrace our love surrounding you, for you are the Chosen One." The Peeps applauded, and I questioned if he just confirmed the fact that Truffle and my Peeps were real. If those words were true, I didn't understand the logic of telling me before the party. Perhaps they believed it would be reassuring to know I'd be returning home to see my loved ones? There was no more time to think when hearing Ulap's boisterous announcement, "From *us* to *you*, it's time for your celebration to begin, so without further ado, let's welcome Sgt. Pepper's Lonely Hearts Club Band!" A feather could have knocked me over when hearing the name of the band. The drapes steadily opened on the stage with flashing blue lights in every direction. Although I couldn't see the band, the reverberating applause from their blaring music was well heard.

Chapter Nineteen

Twist and Shout

THE BAND KICKED OFF THEIR FIRST SONG with bright-pink lights merging with the already flashing blue ones. They swirled round and round, lighting up the spacious club with a magnetic energy. Most of the Peeps hustled to the dance floor while others rushed over in droves to meet me. I was enjoying chatting with them when I spotted Ginor madly waving for me to join him. After trudging my way through the crowd, he introduced me to his friend, Dalni. She was slightly taller than Ginor, with oodles of freckles and strawberry-blonde hair. The three of us were engrossed in chitchat when "Twist and Shout" blasted from their speakers. It was a tune from home which had the same surprising effect as hearing the name of their band. Was it possible the name of that song and the name of their band were brought back to Truffle after they visited Earth? I couldn't resist asking Ginor, "Did you borrow that song and your band name from my planet?" Without hesitation, he replied, "Not guilty!" I certainly had my doubts after observing a most impish look on his face.

Ginor and I set out to mingle with the others, and chatting with them was uplifting. But our chat ended when we stepped back to create a pathway for a long-limbed lady heading our way. She gently wedged her way in front of everyone, and Long Tall Sally introduced herself. She revealed that she had been appointed the chief coordinator in planning my surprise celebration. In a tender tone, she spoke, "We trust you are enjoying your party and we hope it will become a loving memory for you." I nodded but the notion of missing them was such a crushing thought. The conversation soon shifted to why the Peeps vanished from time to time during our adventures. Ms. Sally revealed how they were to sneak off to assist in setting up for my party. At long last, the answer to why they disappeared along our journey was solved! Ironically but much more comically, there was not an ounce of suspense or a bit of drama in the so-called mystery of the vanishing Peeps!

The band members were nicknamed The Peppers and played their planet's songs, yet every so often, I would hear a tune from home. I was trying my best to memorize their melodies and words if I were going home. Of course, only to borrow! Ginor was standing by my side and curiously studying my face. I was confident that he knew of my secret plan. I just looked into his eyes and said, "Don't try to figure out what I'm thinking; just think for yourself!" His speechless look changed to good ole laughter, right along with mine. In the midst of our giggling, we became distracted watching two sisters, Lucille and Anna, hamming it up on the floor. It wasn't long before two more sisters, Carol and Clarabella, trailed behind them, generating their own frivolous moves. It looked like the siblings were trying to outdo one another in some bizarre competition. Ginor remarked they were the masters of The Hippy Hippy Shake, and by their crazy dance moves, no one could dispute that fact. Out of the corner of my eye, I observed Fantebela scrambling her way across the packed floor. She made her way to me, but before she could speak, I asked, "Can you teach me to dance like the sisters?" She grabbed my hand without answering and hustled me to the floor. We invented our own fancy steps when I began feeling guilty many Peeps were waiting to dance with me. I expressed my sentiments to my friend, and she reassured me by announcing, "The night's still young, so be happy just to dance with me, 'cause you know how I'm happy just to dance with you!" I placed my guilt on the back burner, and our creative, fancy moves proceeded to heat up the floor.

After showing off our fancy steps, Fantebela and I hunted for some chairs to catch our breaths. However, we never had the chance to sit down after noticing Ulap strutting toward us. As soon as he arrived, he reached out for my funny-faced friend's hand. She leaned over and whispered in my ear that she was falling in love again. And then off they scurried to the dance floor, hand in hand. I stood spellbound, watching them as they gazed into one another's eyes. Without a moment's notice, Ginor stood before me and broke my spell. He hustled me onto the floor, and as the slow dance shifted to a fast one, we wasted no time flaunting our own original moves. Straight out of my little friend's mouth sprouted a most complimentary comment, "No ands, ifs, or buts, you sure can dig it!" But I wasn't the only one "digging" it. The whole floor vibrated with everyone passionately kicking up their heels.

Chapter Twenty

You Never Give Me Your Money

THE PEPPERS CONTINUED TO PLAY TUNES FROM both planets before announcing they would be taking a short break. After the last note, they stepped off the stage to mingle with their adoring fans. Hojn and his sweetheart, Reemuna, were talking with me when we attempted to see which way the musicians headed. Our search ended in frustration when we lost sight of all of them. However, after a few moments passed, Hojn observed one of the members diagonally across the room. He hollered to him, but to our disappointment, there was no response. He tried again and again, but still no answer. Finally, he shouted in a most piercing voice, "Hey Jude!" And that time, he heard! Jude clamored his way over with Lady Madonna, following in his footsteps. She was rather petite, with kinky red hair, whereas Jude was stocky and bald. The last of the introductions had been set in motion as soon as the remaining two musicians pranced their way over. Hojn proudly announced, "Meet Polythene Pam." I nodded while staring at her golden hair that almost touched the floor.

The last member tilted his head around Pam's shoulder and brandished a sociable nod and blurted, "Howdy, I'm Rocky Raccoon." He was exceptionally rugged, with olive skin and a black beard way past his chin. The introductions had concluded, and the conversation flowed with ease with the talented foursome. However, I couldn't resist questioning myself how their names were just another mysterious coincidence.

We were still immersed in chitchat with The Peppers when several Peeps joined us to praise the talented band. They relentlessly asked the musicians how much longer before they would return to the stage. The answer came from Rocky, who loved the compliment but was frustrated with the same repeated question over and over. Without warning, he left the conversation, stepped up on stage, and headed straight to the microphone. With the strobe lights brightly flashing, only his shadowy figure could be seen. But we could distinctly hear his announcement, "Attention, everybody! Since you never give me your money, they'll be no more entertainment tonight!" Naturally, he was joking, but the mini tykes immediately became teary-eyed. Rocky piped in and announced to the youngsters, "Please don't cry; Uncle Rocky was only teasing." In an instant, their smiles returned to their tiny soaked faces. They looked as if they were beginning to learn teasing was a part of life on Truffle, just like I had too. And once you learn their sense of humor, it gives you one!

The band members soon returned to the stage, and the dance floor once again ignited. It suddenly dawned on me that I had not seen my funny-faced friend in quite some time. I finally spotter her clear across the jam-packed room. The walk to reach her took forever, but I eventually wrangled my way through. She was chatting with two Peeps who looked like mirror images of one another. After reaching them, she excitedly announced, "Meet the biggest fans of The Peppers, Tustar and Tridsa." We cordially shook hands, which predictably turned into hugs. Their effervescent clothes were covered with pictures of The Peppers, and it was abundantly clear how much the siblings adored them. They reminded me of the millions of fans back home who idolized our number one band. The musicians from both of our planets delivered messages of peace through their music, which made sense of how our two worlds collided. It was evident the land of Truffle was filled with so many coincidences. At once, another one hit me like a bolt of lightning; if I were to shuffle the letters in Fantebela's name, it was just another one.

Chapter Twenty-One

Come and Get It!

FANTEBELA, THE SIBLINGS, AND I WERE STILL engaged in our music chatter when we observed a plump gray-haired lady waddling toward the stage. She grabbed the microphone, and in a stern voice, instructed everyone to follow her into the dining room. Fantebela enlightened me that Ms. Julia was their no-nonsense matriarch who just turned sixty-four years old. Time after time, she painstakingly arranges mounds of scrumptious delights for the Peeps to pamper their hungry bellies. Without any humor, I voiced my optimistic feelings to Fantebela, "I hope to still be your friend when I'm sixty-four." Unlike her character, my buddy's demeanor abruptly changed. It was another wake-up call; we would not be part of each other's future. Both of us shook it off and followed the matriarch like she was a five-star general leading us into a top-secret meeting. And like any well-trained soldier of love, we marched together in perfect sync.

After entering the dining room, the matriarch's imposing voice echoed, "Come and get it!" Everyone headed toward the buffet like they hadn't eaten in days and days. The table burst with heaps of lip-smacking vegetables, fruits, and cheeses. It unquestionably was a banquet for royalty. The Peeps kindly stepped aside for me to uphold my regal title of "The Queen Bee." The decorative table reminded me of our picnic where we overstuffed our bellies not long ago. Fantebela and I parked ourselves with Ms. Lizzy and several other famished Peeps.

Nichaty, who was sitting at our table, noticed me squirming in my chair and joshed, "I think you may need two chairs together, Little Queenie." I jokingly replied that if everyone kept stuffing their faces, they would also need two chairs! At the adjoining table, Libly and Nyot overheard our conversation, and their infectious laughter launched a chain reaction throughout the entire room.

After we settled down, the Peeps presented me with bags and bags of goodies for my special day. But there was no opportunity to thank them before recognizing a familiar face advancing toward us. To my astonishment, the notorious Captain stood right before me. He addressed me with his infamous salute, grabbed a chair, and squeezed himself next to me. I sensed my face becoming flushed while I sat frozen in my seat. Once he made himself comfortable, he wasted no time captivating everyone with his amazing tales from the skies. But his stories would end as soon as the announcement of the yummy desserts were ready to be devoured. All eyes were bulging, and all tongues were dangling, looking forward for the sweets to collide with their taste buds. The big hit wasn't the homemade ice cream, the blueberry cheesecake, or even the honey pie. Hands down, it was the wild honey pie that skyrocketed above the others. My mouth overflowed with cheesecake when the Captain leaned over and whispered in my ear, "Please save a dance for me." Surely, my blushing face revealed a most stunned expression as I sat there speechless. He then addressed me with his well-known salute, followed by the renowned clicking of his heels, and once again, he disappeared before my eyes.

With a Little Help from My Friends

The band members were gobbling down their desserts, eager to hustle back on stage before their fans grew too restless. But it wasn't only The Peppers; all the Peeps were devouring their goodies with thoughts of scurrying back to the hall to their dancing feet. That's precisely the time we heard that voice again! The matriarch began waddling over to each table, reprimanding everyone for shoveling down their desserts. It was obvious the Peeps wanted a guaranteed spot on the dance floor and ran like thieves in the night, pretending not to hear her. It was such a comical sight watching them clamber all over each other. At my table, Rabbaar and Cynan eyed one another and then eyeballed the rest of us to devise a plan for our great escape. Almost instantly, the matriarch was suspicious of our scheme to get back to our dancing feet. Not a second passed when we heard her protesting voice shriek, "I've got a feeling that you're all plotting to skedaddle out of here." She obviously knew of our plan, but once she saw our puppy-dog faces, she agreed for us to get moving before she changed her mind. As we were ready to flee, we overheard her say to one of her cronies, "Martha my dear, could you give me a hand in cleaning up?" Her friend politely agreed, and although we were feeling guilty for not helping, nothing could have stopped us from bolting to the dance floor like a wild herd of cattle.

Chapter Twenty-Two

Ooh! My Soul

WE WERE OVERJOYED RETURNING TO THE DANCE floor where the rock and roll music burst through the speakers. The Peeps soon initiated a chant for their legendary crooner, Mr. Moonlight, to serenade his much-loved Maggie Mae. He gladly consented to their request and trotted to the stage, shouting, "I love you, Mag!"

She sweetly and cleverly responded, "I love you to the moon and back, Moony!" He smiled while commanding the stage with self-confidence.

In no time, his raspy voice belted out loud and clear to her, "I wanna be your man!" Although Maggie nervously blushed, she relished in the fact that he was sharing his love with her on stage. It was just another song from home, yet hearing the known as well as the unknown no longer fazed me. As soon as Moonlight sang the last note, he stepped off the stage, accompanied by the noise of the shattering applause. He took a bow and blew kisses while receiving a standing ovation.

Before The Peppers commenced playing again, Jude asked if anyone else would like to step on stage to sing. A weepy youngster raised his hand, and all heads tilted to see a miniature fella bawling away. He couldn't remember what the name of the song was, and his tears steadily streamed down his face. Jude reassured him, "Please don't cry, your mother should know."

The pint-sized Enil glanced at his mom, and she cried out to him, "It's 'Somewhere over the Rainbow'!" The little tyke wiped his eyes and anxiously scooted to the stage to sing yet another one of my planet's treasured songs. The crowd listened to him flawlessly belt out the melodious tune, and after the last note, he darted back into the whistling crowd.

Out of the blue, my name unexpectedly blared out of the loudspeakers. The Peeps politely cleared the floor, and to my sheer disbelief, he appeared once again before me. My handsome Captain bowed and reached for my hand. I trusted not to collapse, hearing my inside voice screaming, "Ooh, my heart! Ooh! My soul!" His words to save a dance for him had come true. I courteously accepted his offer, and we waltzed together with elegance and grace. Visibly, there was no question of who happened to be the "Belle of the Ball." After our flawless dance, the Peeps applauded and blew kisses. My captain then escorted me to my abandoned throne and affectionately kissed my hand. Not a word was spoken, yet the sentiments we shared were unmistakably obvious. I thought I saw a tear, but I assumed it had to be my imagination. Nonetheless, our time had abruptly ended, and as customary, he saluted, clicked his heels, and faded out of sight. I sat motionless while feeling powerless to battle the empty void in my heart.

My thoughts were scattered, trying to make sense of anything and everything. I reflected to when my world was a bleak gray and how it changed into a sunny yellow. But what about tomorrow? Will I wake up on Truffle to discover everything to be real? Or will I wake up in my bed to find everything to be a dream? My mind began to wander, but once I witnessed hundreds of bubbly faces dancing away, I decided that I don't want to spoil the party. I placed my heart-shaped glasses on, grabbed my bags of goodies to share with my friends, and paraded to the dance floor. Within no time, I changed into a bubbly face too!

Chapter Twenty-Three

Sexy Sadie

THE FESTIVITIES CARRIED ON, EXCEPT FOR AN occasional yawn from the children and grandparents. Hojn had been keeping me company when a ballad called "12-Bar Original" channeled through the amplifiers. Not only was I aware of its origin, but I had become accustomed to hearing songs again and again from my planet. After it ended, both Hojn and I ventured to find Roggee but were stopped dead in our tracks hearing Madonna's voice pipe through the speakers, "This jitterbug is for you Blue!" Out of the crowd, a long-limbed character named Blue strutted to the floor, flaunting his blue hat, his blue bowtie, and his blue suede shoes. Evidently, it was no secret how he was blessed with that nickname. Every one of us became entranced watching him jitterbug to the likes of no other. How he managed to blow kisses to his beloved Koyo while at the same time kicking up his heels was pure magic. Apparently, the Peeps also seized the opportunity to bring our jitterbug to Truffle. If I were dreaming, I had no control of it, and if it were reality, the answer was the same.

In next to no time, bright lights sprang forth on a colorful assortment of tropical trees. A crew of grandma cronies sashayed to the floor dressed in flamboyant costumes and stylish hats. Each one resembled a giddy teenager performing the most unconventional of dances. In a flash, they stole the show right out from under Blue's nose. My eyes were fixated on the frolicking grannies when Fantebela grabbed my hand and steered me to the floor to accompany them. Ginor and his buddy, Rabni, followed in our footsteps, and the four of us had no trouble showing off our fancy footwork. Everybody was dancing away when I predicted it was just a matter of time before the grandmothers would gradually run out of steam. My hunch proved right, watching them quietly exit the floor one by one. Not long after, the same fate occurred when Ginor and his buddy eventually lost their momentum and marched off. Only a matter of seconds flew by before Fantebela and I dug into our stored energy and miraculously transformed into The Main Event. We were quite the sensation *until* that sexy Sadie gal made her grand entrance. The spotlight cast a shadow over us, whereas a glaring one ignited above Sadie. In a fleeting moment, Fantebela and I lost everyone's attention, just like Blue lost his to the grandmas! We scrambled off the floor, listening to the roaring crowd cheer for Sadie, and turned into shadowy spectators like everybody else.

Sadie's fiery red dress and glittering red heels were causing a massive uproar throughout the room. Her unorthodox moves lit up the hall, like sizzling fireworks. The only words that could be heard throughout the room were, "Go, Sadie, Go!" There was not a doubt how she adored being the center of attention. Ginor reunited with Fantebela and me, and the three of us continued to watch Sadie's mesmerizing steps. My funny-faced friend muttered she would be just as sexy as Sadie if she dressed like her. After that remark, I leaned to Ginor and whispered, "She sure is sexy!"

Fantebela piped right in, "Are you talking about me?"

After winking at Ginor, I responded, "Of course, I'm talking about you!" She quickly realized I was referring to Sadie, and predictably, another funny face sprang into view. In the meantime, my eyes remained fastened on Sadie's unpredicted moves. I anticipated those fancy steps of hers would be coming with me if I were returning home to Memphis, Tennessee. But more than anything, what I really wanted to bring home were my little friends.

Chapter Twenty-Four

You Like Me Too Much

ALTHOUGH ROGGEE HAD BEEN MISSING FOR A long, long, long time, I knew our promise to dance together would have never been broken. After I searched the hall, I caught sight of him conversing with a stylish-looking lady and a distinguished-looking gentleman. I maneuvered my way over where my friend planted a heartfelt peck on my cheek. He then introduced me to his gal, Tepita, and his gentleman friend, Maxwell. According to Roggee, Max was their life-saving carpenter on Truffle, and there wasn't a solitary thing he wasn't capable of building or repairing. At all times, his tools were nearby, but it was his silver hammer that always clung to his side. There were swirling rumors Max slept with his prized possession, and if for some reason his hammer was lost and then found, everyone would know it was Maxwell's silver hammer! Although Max was relentlessly teased, he didn't mind the banter; in fact, he loved it. He thoughtfully said to me, "Please let me know if you ever need anything built or repaired."

I kindly replied, "Thank you, but I believe I'm only passing through!"

Roggee, retorted, "Not if I get my way!"

He nodded when I responded, "I think you like me too much!" He reached out for my hand, and we headed to the dance floor. Needless to say, I was sure it was just another last dance.

Once the music ended, Roggee escorted me to my neglected throne. Prior to him walking away, he assured me we would see each other again before the night was over. I thought, not only was my party ending, but the same fate would soon be taking place with my little friends. I sat in silence to capture a few moments, but my somber thoughts were interrupted once the band proclaimed the next tune was an all-time favorite. After listening to the first few chords, I nearly toppled out of my royal chair. There was no disputing "The Ballad of John and Yoko" was my planet's song and when hearing it, I believed I had been hurled into another dimension. Meanwhile, my queen's seat and I were stuck together while breathlessly waiting for the next bombshell. And it wasn't just one bombshell; it was an assortment of them! "Komm, Gib Mir Deine Hand, Besame Mucho and Sie Liebt Dich." Ulap's words of visiting Earth during peaceful times had convinced me that the music from my planet was undeniably brought back to Truffle. But the same haunting question still arose, was it the wildest of dreams or the craziest of reality? I tried to place my thoughts on the back burner, but I already knew it was a losing battle.

Chapter Twenty-Five

A Shot of Rhythm and Blues

MY REGAL CHAIR AND I WERE STILL attached to one another when hearing yet another tune from my planet called "The Honeymoon Song." After the last note, The Peppers stepped off the stage to mingle, except Jude, who proceeded to walk toward me. I believed he knew my thoughts, and as he drew closer, my body remained glued to my chair, and my perplexed expression remained glued to my face. But before I could speak, he stated, "We know and love all your songs, especially the ones symbolizing love and peace."

At that moment, I realized he knew my thoughts, and I straightforwardly asked, "How do you do it?" He assured me that it wasn't him, but it was some other guy nicknamed JoJo that travels to Earth to borrow our treasured songs. Remarkably, Jude began rattling off every country, and before he could come up for a breath of air, his last words were "even back in the USSR!" He apparently was no longer aware it was called the USSR, but at last I learned how my planet's music found their way to Truffle. It didn't take long for me to realize that not only our songs, but some of our names, our dances, and our ball games were also borrowed.

A new conversation sprung up when a young gal wandered over and bashfully spoke, "Hi, Uncle Jude!" A whopping smile appeared on his face as he twirled her around and around. Glowing with pride, he introduced me to Mary Jane, his freckle-faced niece. Jude informed me The Peppers would be playing the following night at her Sweet Little Sixteen party next door at the Saturday Club.

Jude teasingly said to her, "Wow, sixteen tomorrow! What's the new Mary Jane going to look like?" She blushed and said she'd still be the same ole Mary Jane she'd always been. Jude reminded her, not only was it her special day, but it was The Saturday Club's special day as well. With the anticipation of celebrating both events, he playfully announced, "Happy Birthday Dear Saturday Club, and also a very happy one to Mary Jane!" It dawned on me that there was never a mention of tomorrow night's festivities. My conclusion was simple; I would not be present for either one.

The Peppers returned to the stage as their high-spirited fans clapped and cheered for them. Yet before playing, we heard Madonna broadcast on the mic, "Everyone, get on the floor and shake, rattle and roll those booties!" I watched with Hojn as the Peeps raced to the floor like a stampede of elephants. In a flash, both of us ran as fast as our legs could carry us to find a corner spot to stay alive! Shortly thereafter, a well-proportioned gal made her way to the floor and began shimmying. Her brother, Johnny B. Goode, followed her and attempted to vibrate his hips by trying to imitate his sister but with no luck.

We all chuckled listening to him grumble, "I wish I could shimmy like my sister Kate!" After he kept trying over and over, he finally gave up.

With a Little Help from My Friends

    The pulsating floor overflowed with the Peeps dancing to the beat of the music. Hojn and I were surviving in our corner spot when I was overcome with a premonition somebody was sure to fall. But it wouldn't have been too far since we were all crunched together, like sardines. That hunch of mine came true when witnessing sweet Georgia Brown topple over. She created a massive pile-up, with countless others tumbling on top of her. The poor thing was being smothered but still managed to shriek, "Please get me out of here!"

    Her friend, Nubro, heard her cries and profusely began stuttering, "She said she said, get me outa here, get me outa here!" Scores of us ran to her aid and to the other unfortunate Peeps who were being buried under the giant heap. Their assorted shades of rainbow clothes were mingled together, looking like a psychedelic kaleidoscope.

    The disheveled Ms. Brown, along with the other stunned Peeps, were being rescued when we heard a voice shouting, "Where's my baby? I got to find my baby!" Once hearing those words from his dad's lips, the dazed Rumyar leaped up from the giant pile. After a hug from his father, he darted back to the jam-packed floor as if nothing happened, and so did everyone else.

    The dancing was in full force, but when the music ended, the lights grew dim. The floor was cleared, and the decorated table was wheeled in together with a heart-shaped multicolored cake. The candles sparkled in every direction and lit up the massive hall. Everyone burst into singing, and I inhaled my deepest breath, blowing out the candles, hoping for my wish to come true. We devoured the cake in minutes, and the floor immediately returned to life. Everyone was stomping their feet and waving their arms like they were communicating in some strange sign language. I chuckled to myself thinking they must have visited Doc Robert before the party and was given a shot of rhythm and blues.

Chapter Twenty-Six

You've Got to Hide Your Love Away

THE ENTHUSIASM IN THE HALL FIZZLED THE moment The Peppers revealed their next song would be their last. The band members looked into my eyes and began singing "I'll Be Seeing You." It was another song from home which I believed was chosen especially for me. After the final note, The Peppers stepped off the stage and headed my way. They formed a circle around me, and each one waited their turn for a hug. We shared smiles when I professed my love for all their music, no matter where it originated. Almost immediately, I noticed everyone saying good night to one another and understood it was just a matter of time. All the sad-faced Peeps began parading my way for that one last embrace. I became paralyzed with chilling thoughts of my future, but somehow, I managed to maintain my composure. With a deep sigh, I spoke, "Thank you for being the most loving and gracious hosts."

Neja, Ratheeh and Mya, the junior coordinators, offered the same complementary words, "Thank you for being the most loving and gracious guest!"

I respectfully replied, "That means a lot to me, and all of you mean the world to me, both worlds."

Fantebela and Ulap were also bidding their farewells to everyone, and I realized we would be departing at any moment. Likewise, I assumed Hojn, Roggee, and Ginor would also be saying their goodbyes, but they were nowhere to be found. However, after a few moments, several taps were placed on my shoulder, and to my sheer delight, it was none other than my three monkeys. Their arms encircled me, and I could feel the power of their love warming my body. It surely had to be the tightest group hug across the universe, but it made no sense. Weren't they coming with Ulap, Fantebela, and me? I suddenly grasped the dreaded fact they were not. The notion of never seeing my monkeys again was beyond devastating. An overwhelming sense of sadness swept over me, yet in some miraculous way, I put on a brave face and concealed the sinking feeling in the pit of my stomach. There are moments you've got to hide your love away, so without creating an emotional scene, I reached for Ulap's and Fantebela's hands. The three of us walked into the night, but I was the only one who was walking into the unknown.

Chapter Twenty-Seven

A Day in the Life

HAVING FANTEBELA AND ULAP BY MY SIDE consoled me, but sorrow lingered in my heart without my monkeys. Not a word was spoken as we trudged on, yet the silence was deafening. The full moon and Lucy's sparkling diamonds guided us along the path when unexpectedly, my funny-faced friend vanished without a trace. Ulap and I frantically searched for her and found her nestled on the ground behind some trees. She seemed to be in a spellbinding daze, and I thought maybe she was trying to hide her love away, just like me. I believed the three of us knew our time together was drawing closer and closer. To ease the somber mood, I jokingly said to Ulap, "You better keep *all* your eyes open or you're going to lose that girl of yours!" He politely laughed while confessing he was also carrying a burden of sorrow. We then helped my funny-faced friend pick herself up. As she dusted herself off, we all looked at one another, and a thousand things were said without a single word.

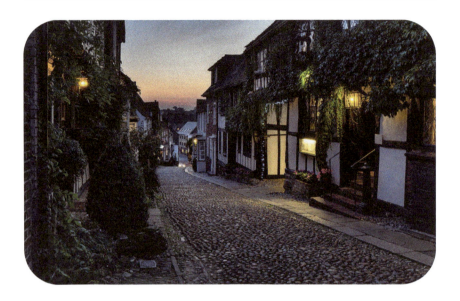

We reached their moonlit neighborhood before turning a corner onto Penny Lane. A flagstone bridge appeared, and as we crossed, I welcomed the gentle sounds of a brook below, delivering music to my ears. Once we crossed the bridge, several quaint cottages appeared in full view. Multicolored flowers not only bordered their walkways but also lined their cobblestone streets. After viewing one of the fairy-tale cottages, it was no real secret who resided there. The walkway looked like the game board from Candyland, brightening their home along with its cherry-pink shutters. Their colorful flower boxes and their iridescent lights peeking through the shrubs took my breath away. It was a genuine fairyland that only imaginations and dreams created. Ulap announced with pride, "Welcome to our home!" It appeared welcoming, until I visualized their spaceship may be hiding in their backyard. I tried setting those thoughts aside as Fantebela proudly began escorting me on a tour of their fairylike residence. Meanwhile, Ulap scooted off to the kitchen to prepare hot chocolate for us. Their home radiated a feeling of tranquility until my friend steered me to the backdoor. As the door steadily creaked open, a sense of panic rushed over me. I grabbed her hand with no intention of letting go, and in seconds, loud, rustling sounds were heard. There was no spaceship, but to my shock, hiding behind some bushes were my three irreplaceable monkeys! Roggee confessed they ran as fast as their little legs could carry them to arrive before us. My funny-faced friend succeeded in surprising me again, and my mood happily shifted. There was no containing myself as I shouted at the top of my lungs, "Hallelujah, I love her so!" Likewise, my monkeys also agreed that to know her is to love her.

Once we all settled down, Ulap delighted everyone with the hot chocolate he fondly prepared for us. Their calming room overflowed with photographs of their fellow Peeps, as well as pictures of their magical Truffle. We congregated on the floor and gathered on some oversized pillows. Ginor suddenly sprang up, performing his soft-shoe shuffle while keeping the jolly mood going. After his shuffle, he plopped himself down and recalled how the both of us were quite the sensation *until* that Sadie gal stole our spotlight. Hojn piped right in and recapped how his parakeet flew away the second I began singing. Fantebela waited her turn to recount my horrified look catching her fly ball only to watch it slowly roll out of my hands. More giggling followed as Roggee reminded everyone of my shocked face when he wandered from the fields, behaving like a madman, singing a wacky jingle about a monkey. But the biggest laugh of all was the moment Ulap chimed in by reminding everyone how my tripping had become part of my daily routine. He affectionately announced, "Even though your feet's too big, we know that your heart is much bigger!"

The evening drifted into the wee hours of the morning, together with loads and loads of laughter. We prolonged every moment, reminiscing our escapades, beginning with the visit with Ms. M and the children. We proceeded to recap the time we shared on the submarine, the picnic, the cave, the safari, the ball game, the balloon ride, and my surprise party. My sincerest words were expressed. "I want to tell you all the things we did today and all the things we said today have filled my heart with more love than one could ever imagine. Throughout our journey, we were all together, just like we are all together now, and each one of you have made me feel like Christmas time is here again." They stared at me with voiceless faces while heartbroken tears streamed down mine. Fantebela then lifted herself from her pillow and reached out for my hand. Our departure from the room had been set in motion. With a struggling wave, I turned around and sighed to Ulap and my monkeys, "See you in the morning." At least that's what I told myself.

The rose and lavender colors in the bedroom provided a comforting feeling, yet the unknown was anything but comforting. I shared with Fantebela what a special day it was for me, and how I didn't want it to end. She replied, "Just remember, it's always the little things that can brighten a day, soften a heart, and create a smile. Never forget the little things are limitless. Continue with that smile on your face and kindness in your heart as new adventures will soon begin. You never know what might unfold and who you may see in the future." I seated myself on the bed, and my friend jumped right on with me. She tried her best to cheer me up with her funny faces, and before I knew it, I found myself making funny faces too! We giggled like little kids trying to capture every second of what may be our last night with one another. She expressed how much fun we always *have* together, and I blurted out, "Ditto." That's when it dawned on me that she didn't say *had* together; she said *have* together. Did that mean we would be seeing each other in the morning? The words lingered on the tip of my tongue to ask, but I was afraid to hear the answer. At last, I gathered the courage and optimistically asked, "Will we have time to make some funny faces tomorrow?" Her expression changed as she tried to speak, but there were no words, only tears. She kissed my forehead, walked out of the room, and I was sure, out of my life.

The void inside me was no mystery, but whether a dream or reality certainly was. What goes on in your mind can cause such confusion when trying to make sense of the senseless. I questioned, if I were already sleeping, then how could I go to sleep? Can you dream within a dream? Where would I be tomorrow? After many twists and turns, I tried reassuring myself when the dawn breaks, Ulap will be making hot chocolate, my three monkeys will be hiding, and Fantebela will be making funny faces. Within seconds, my eyes became exceptionally heavy, and I could feel myself drifting off. The very last thing I remembered, what a day in the life with my little friends.

Chapter Twenty-Eight

Lonesome Tears in My Eyes

THE CRASHING SOUNDS OF THUNDER THAT AWAKENED me yesterday morning, I heard all over again. Confusion and sadness consumed me when I opened my eyes and found myself in my own bed. There was no Ulap making hot chocolate, there were no monkeys hiding, there was no Fantebela making funny faces…there was no Truffle. Was it conceivable I just experienced one of the most extraordinary dreams that anyone could ever imagine? Yet I refused to believe that my little friends did not exist and believed, at any moment, they'd be back for me. But after waiting, waiting, and waiting, there would be no one. Hope was replaced with hopelessness, knowing I would forever be fixing a hole in my heart. At last, the thunder stopped, but the battering rain continued to hammer against my window. With enormous effort, I pulled myself up from my bed and dragged myself into the bathroom. While starring in my mirror, I irrationally blurted out, "I'm looking through you, and I'm looking at you." But what was I looking for or what was I looking at? Perhaps a carbon copy of my little friends? Shockingly, what I did see in my mirror's reflection was a ghost-like figure of Fantebela scaring me half to death as she came in through the bathroom window. But as fast as she appeared was as fast as she disappeared! I frantically searched for her, but she was gone, like a thief in the night! I should have known better; it was only an apparition, and a gigantic wave of grief rushed over me as I lost my little girl.

With a Little Help from My Friends

Unsteadily, I stumbled into the kitchen where my reliable coffee pot was waiting for me. With a case of the blues, I said to myself, "I'm gonna sit right down and cry and let the lonesome tears in my eyes join me and my coffee. That's all I can do, that's all I've got to do." There was no telling how much time passed before picking myself up and staggering into my living room. I curled up on my window seat where the loving memories of my friends refused to leave me alone. As the hours passed, the bleak day faded into darkness. After mustering up some energy, I headed to my bedroom, attempting to escape, just like dreamers do. As my weary body crawled into bed, I wished for the power to turn back the clock to the night before. Closing my eyes, I whispered to Ulap, "I call your name, but you don't answer." Then I sighed to Fantebela. "I need you, but you don't respond." After a deep breath, more wishful words were spoken. "Please come back for me; I know we can work it out." Only dead silence was heard, and an unwelcomed resentment surfaced while feeling like they abandoned me. But after some thought, "I decided,

I'll cry instead of remaining so angry." Although I'm down, my life will carry on, but it will never be the same without my little friends. My once colorful world turned colorless.

Chapter Twenty-Nine

Crying, Waiting, Hoping

AFTER A HARD DAY'S NIGHT, THE BRIGHT sun rays flooded through my window early in the morning. With every ounce of my being, I struggled to face the new day by shouting, "Good day sunshine!" Trying to convince myself I feel fine was my optimistic expectation. It wasn't very long before the postman and I spotted one another. He advanced toward my mailbox, flashing a jovial smile and a friendly wave. I politely returned his wave, and as soon as he walked away, I strolled to the box to grab some bills and a notice from the dreaded taxman. It just happened to be another rude awakening that my real world had resumed. Walking back in, I tossed the mail on my table, picked up my neglected guitar, and moseyed back outside. I seated myself on my old-fashioned creaky porch swing, and after playing hours upon hours, the night gradually crept up. Once again, I proceeded to my bedroom with those same wishful thoughts of becoming a beautiful dreamer.

Regrettably, there were no sweet dreams for me, and the new morning presented itself with the same monotonous routine. It had become a constant struggle to face the realization that my friends and Truffle had only been a dream. But my sixth sense disagreed. After all, wasn't I their chosen one? Wasn't I the one to spread peace and love? The notion that they changed their minds thinking I'm a loser and wasn't competent to fulfill their wish was unimaginable. The time had come for me to grasp the fact it had all been a dream and realize my sixth sense was sadly mistaken. It was also time to move on and convince myself all things *will* pass. With a great deal of conviction, I reassured myself all things *must* pass. But deep down inside, I still believed my only answer was crying, waiting, hoping.

With a Little Help from My Friends

More days dragged on with endless mornings and countless nights sliding into one another. The tracking of time had become lost, and for all I knew, there could have been eight days a week. My family and friends believed I was in seclusion, writing my next mystery novel. I laughed thinking they should only know the real mystery. My guitar had become my best friend, offering me some comfort and solace. While sitting on my porch, strumming away, I caught a glimpse of my smiling postman once again. My disheartened mood kicked in, and I shouted, "Mailman, bring me no more blues! I'm so tired of all the junk mail!" He looked straight at me with a most startled expression. Feeling dreadful, I gave out another shout, "Please Mister Postman, excuse my rude manners!"

With a deep Southern drawl, he responded, "I just don't understand, ma'am! Do yer got those yer blues?"

I hollered, "Yeah, my guitar and me got those blues, and while my guitar gently weeps, so do I!" His stunned face stared right at me, and then off he flew into a madcap dash.

Although my behavior was alarming, I immediately dismissed it when I observed a colorful envelope that he tossed in the mailbox. And that's precisely the moment it all began to unravel! The colorful envelope reminded me of my little friends and their multicolored world. It brought back all the memories that I desperately needed to forget. My first reaction was to rip it up to prevent further ones from surfacing, but the bold-faced letters prohibited me from doing just that. Suddenly, I was feeling lightheaded when the letters punched me in the face, like a prizefighter just K.O.d me. In the upper left-hand corner, TRUFFLE.

Chapter Thirty

A Beginning

MY NERVES WERE RATTLED, AND MY BREATHING labored as I staggered back inside and collapsed in my kitchen chair. If I needed someone, it was at that moment. With my deepest breath yet, my trembling hands gently and methodically opened the envelope. After what seemed like an eternity, I unfolded a piece of paper with a photograph tucked inside. The photo fell onto my lap—right along with *reality*. I wiped my tears that were blurring my vision, but the image remained. Feeling paralyzed and euphoric at the same time, I tried to compose myself by taking more deep breaths so that my pounding heart wouldn't jump out of my chest. I placed the priceless picture next to me and began to read every word written on the precious paper from which it fell.

Dear Prudence,

Hello little girl. Although this letter is from me to you, we all miss you with heavy hearts. Fantebela especially misses your laughter and the many funny faces you shared. There is not a day that goes by that Ginor, Roggee, and Hojn do not speak of you with so much love, but it's this boy who feels like a nowhere man without you.

We had no idea who would be The Chosen One, till there was you. We were saddened by your dark mood, but with your genuine heart and beautiful soul, we knew it had to be you. Yes it is you in whom we have boundless faith, it is you who will bring kindness into your world, and it is you who will inspire others to follow. After spending so many treasured moments together, we have confidence your spirit will return. Perhaps there will come a day we shall meet again.

Please know there's a place in our hearts for you that will forever live on, and our loving friendship will be cherished through all eternity. Believe with all your heart that peace, kindness, and love can be possible someday. Although you won't see me, I will eternally be, right beside you.

All my loving,
Ulap

P.S. I love you.

There it was, in black and white. My pleading voice echoed. "I've got to get you into my life again." But I knew my words were all in vain. As I read the letter over and over, I refused to give up that glimmer of hope that one day we may meet again. The sorrow of missing them was heartbreaking, yet knowing my time with my friends had not been a dream created the most peaceful inner feeling. As I sat in silence, the sun's rays streamed through my window, shining brighter and brighter. I walked over, and when I peered out, the most spectacular rainbow appeared. Remarkably, that same miraculous calmness swept through me as it had once before. With a new burst of energy, I could sense their presence and feel them surrounding me with pure love.

Perhaps, my new mystery novel will be called *Now and Then*, written in honor of some beautiful souls that altered my belief that kindness, peace, and love may well be possible one day. With my friends' welcomed guidance, my quest shall begin. The truths of all truths were Ulap's words, "Baby, you're a rich man, not by your possessions, but by the love you share with others." Tomorrow never knows, but with a little help from my friends, my mission will begin, knowing they will be with me every step of the way. Was this the end? No, it was a beginning.

Answers in Chapters

CHAPTER ONE

Run for Your Life

Misery
Not A Second Time
Paperback Writer
Chains
Wait
Golden Slumbers
Tell Me What You See
I've Just Seen a Face
In My Life
I'm Only Sleeping
Run for Your Life
Something

CHAPTER TWO

You Really Got a Hold on Me

Boys
I Saw Her Standing There
Girl
Thank You Girl
Ob-La-Di-Ob-La-Da
Words of Love
Little Child
Hello, Goodbye
You Really Got a Hold on Me
No Reply
Free As a Bird

When I Get Home
Glass Onion
Helter Skelter
Every Little Thing
It's All Too Much
I Want to Hold Your Hand
Two of Us
Slow Down

CHAPTER THREE

Step Inside Love

The Inner Light
Step Inside Love
Here, There and Everywhere
Good Morning Good Morning
She's Leaving Home
Ask Me Why
Strawberry Fields Forever
Within You Without You
Because

CHAPTER FOUR

Don't Pass Me By

Blue Jay Way
Kansas City
Old Brown Shoe
Don't Pass Me By

Doctor Robert

CHAPTER FIVE

Glad All Over

Michelle
Young Blood
Glad All Over
Teddy Boy
Roll Over Beethoven
Being for the Benefit of Mr. Kite
The Continuing Story
of Bungalow Bill

CHAPTER SIX

Getting Better

Pepperland
It Won't Be Long
The Word
Getting Better
Let It Be
The Long and Winding Road
Too Much Monkey Business
September in the Rain
Yellow Submarine
Honey Don't
Devil in Her Heart
She Loves You
And I Love Her
Three Cool Cats
The Sheik Of Araby

The Palace of the
King of the Birds
Matchbox

CHAPTER SEVEN

Magical Mystery Tour

Yellow Submarine in Pepperland
Help
In Spite Of All the Danger
If I Fell
Hold Me Tight
Day Tripper
That'll Be the Day
Do You Want to Know a Secret
Sour Milk Sea
Sea of Monsters
I Am the Walrus
Oh! Darling
Please Please Me
Pepperland Laid Waste
Sea of Holes
Sea of Time
Norwegian Wood
Love of the Loved
Lovely Rita
What You're Doing
Everybody's Trying
to Be My Baby
Magical Mystery Tour
Tell Me Why

CHAPTER EIGHT

Here Comes the Sun

The Fool on the Hill
She's a Woman
Dizzy Miss Lizzy
March of the Meanies
Here Comes the Sun
Sun King
Savoy Truffle
Ain't She Sweet
Love Me Do
Another Girl
Real Love

CHAPTER NINE

I'll Follow the Sun

Carry That Weight
I'll Follow the Sun
Cayenne
I Me Mine
Where Have You
Been All My Life

CHAPTER TEN

A Taste of Honey

Heather
Why Don't We Do
It in the Road

Eleanor Rigby
A Taste of Honey
Blackbird
And Your Bird Can Sing
Dig a Pony
Mother Nature's Son
Hey Bulldog
Leave My Kitten Alone
Take Good Care of My Baby
Don't Let Me Down
One and One Is Two
One After 909
Child of Nature
Everybody's Got Something
to Hide Except Me
and My Monkey
For No One
Don't Ever Change

CHAPTER ELEVEN

All You Need Is Love

Keep Your Hands Off My Baby
Catswalk
Can't Buy Me Love
All You Need Is Love

CHAPTER TWELVE

Act Naturally

Piggies
Circles

Drive My Car
I Forgot to Remember to Forget
Act Naturally
That's All Right
I'll Be on My Way

CHAPTER THIRTEEN

Nothing Shakin'

Nothin' Shakin'
Watching Rainbows
Happiness Is a Warm Gun
Bad Boy
Bad to Me
So How Come

CHAPTER FOURTEEN

Baby's In Black

Take Out Some Insurance on Me Baby
I Want You
You Can't Do That
Revolution 1
Revolution 9
Revolution
Baby's In Black
You'll Be Mine
I Got a Woman

CHAPTER FIFTEEN

Ticket to Ride

Mean Mr. Mustard
I'll Get You
Don't Bother Me
Ticket to Ride
Cry For a Shadow
Cry Baby Cry
I'll Be Back

CHAPTER SIXTEEN

It's Only Love

Money
Flying
Anytime at All
Octopus's Garden
My Bonnie
Lend Me Your Comb
You Know What to Do
If You've Got Trouble
Searchin'
It's Only Love
Goodbye

CHAPTER SEVENTEEN

Baby It's You

Only a Northern Song
Moonlight Bay

Lucy in the Sky with Diamonds
Baby It's You
Birthday

CHAPTER EIGHTEEN

Come Together

Come Together
Carnival of Light
Her Majesty
You Know My Name
I Remember You
Commonwealth
From Us to You
Sgt. Pepper's Lonely
Heart's Club Band

CHAPTER NINETEEN

Twist and Shout

Twist and Shout
Not Guilty
Long Tall Sally
Think for Yourself
Lucille
Anna
Carol
Clarabella
The Hippy Hippy Shake
I'm Happy Just to
Dance with You
Falling in Love Again

Dig It

CHAPTER TWENTY

You Never Give Me Your Money

Hey Jude
Lady Madonna
Polythene Pam
Rocky Raccoon
You Never Give Me Your Money
The Walk

CHAPTER TWENTY-ONE

Come and Get It

Julia
When I'm Sixty-Four
Soldier of Love
Come and Get It
Little Queenie
Honey Pie
Wild Honey Pie
Get Back
I've Got a Feeling
Martha My Dear

CHAPTER TWENTY-TWO

Oh! My Soul

Rock and Roll Music
Mr. Moonlight
Maggie Mae
Love You To
I Wanna Be Your Man
Your Mother Should Know
Ooh! My Soul
Belle of the Ball
I Don't Want to Spoil the Party

CHAPTER TWENTY-THREE

Sexy Sadie

12-Bar Original
For You Blue
Blue Suede Shoes
Sexy Sadie
I'm Talking About You
Memphis, Tennessee

CHAPTER TWENTY-FOUR

You Like Me Too Much

Long, Long, Long
Maxwell's Silver Hammer
You Like Me Too Much
The Ballad of John and Yoko
Komm, Gib Mir Deine Hand
Besame Mucho
Sie Liebt Dich

CHAPTER TWENTY-FIVE

A Shot Of Rhythm and Blues

The Honeymoon Song
How Do You Do It
Some Other Guy
Back in the USSR
Sweet Little Sixteen
What's the New Mary Jane
Happy Birthday Dear
Saturday Club
Shake, Rattle and Roll
Johnny B. Goode
I Wish I Could Shimmy Like My Sister Kate
Sure to Fall
Sweet Georgia Brown
She Said She Said
I Got to Find My Baby
A Shot Of Rhythm & Blues

CHAPTER TWENTY-SIX

You've Got to Hide Your Love Away

Good Night
That Means a Lot
Across the Universe
You've Got to Hide Your Love Away

CHAPTER TWENTY-SEVEN

A Day in the Life

You're Going to Lose That Girl
Penny Lane
Hallelujah, I Love Her So
To Know Her Is to Love Her
Madman
Your Feet's Too Big
Reminiscing
I Want to Tell You
Things We Said Today
All Together Now
Christmas Time Is Here Again
Tip of My Tongue
What Goes On
A Day in the Life

CHAPTER TWENTY-EIGHT

Lonesome Tears in My Eyes

Yesterday
Fixing a Hole
Rain
I'm Looking Through You
She Came in Through the Bathroom Window
I Should Have Known Better
I Lost My Little Girl
A Case of the Blues

I'm Gonna Sit Right Down and Cry
Lonesome Tears in My Eyes
All I've Got to Do
Like Dreamers Do
The Night Before
I Call Your Name
I Need You
We Can Work It Out
I'll Cry Instead
I'm Down

CHAPTER TWENTY-NINE

Crying, Waiting, Hoping

A Hard Day's Night
Early in the Morning
Good Day Sunshine
I Feel Fine
Taxman
Beautiful Dreamer
I'm a Loser
All Things Must Pass
Crying, Waiting, Hoping
Eight Days a Week
Mailman Bring Me No More Blues
I'm So Tired
Junk
Shout
Please Mister Postman
I Just Don't Understand
Yer Blues

While My Guitar Genlty Weeps
Rip It Up

CHAPTER THIRTY

A Beginning

If I Needed Someone
Dear Prudence
Hello Little Girl
From Me to You
This Boy
Nowhere Man
Till There Was You
Yes It Is
There's a Place
You Won't See Me
I Will
All My Loving
P.S. I Love You
Got to Get You into My Life
Now and Then
Baby You're a Rich Man
Tomorrow Never Knows
With a Little Help
From My Friends
The End
A Beginning

Song Titles in Alphabetical Order

SONG TITLES	CHAPTER
12-Bar Original	23
A Beginning	30
A Case of the Blues	28
A Day in the Life	27
A Hard Day's Night	29
A Shot Of Rhythm and Blues	25
A Taste of Honey	10
Across the Universe	26
Act Naturally	12
Ain't She Sweet	08
All I've Got to Do	28
All My Loving	30
All Things Must Pass	29
All Together Now	27
All You Need Is Love	11
And I Love Her	06
And Your Bird Can Sing	10
Anna	19
Another Girl	08
Anytime at All	16
Ask Me Why	03
Baby It's You	17
Baby You're a Rich Man	30
Baby's In Black	14
Back in the USSR	25
Bad Boy	13
Bad to Me	13

Beautiful Dreamer	29
Because	03
Being for the Benefit of Mr. Kite	05
Belle of the Ball	22
Besame Mucho	24
Birthday	17
Blackbird	10
Blue Jay Way	04
Blue Suede Shoes	23
Boys	02
Can't Buy Me Love	11
Carnival of Light	18
Carol	19
Carry That Weight	09
Catswalk	11
Cayenne	09
Chains 01	01
Child of Nature	10
Christmas Time Is Here Again	27
Circles	12
Clarabella	19
Come and Get It	21
Come Together	18
Commonwealth	18
Cry Baby Cry	15
Cry For a Shadow	15
Crying, Waiting, Hoping	29
Day Tripper	07
Dear Prudence	30
Devil in Her Heart	06
Dig a Pony	10

Dig It	19
Dizzy Miss Lizzy	08
Do You Want to Know a Secret	07
Doctor Robert	04
Don't Bother Me	15
Don't Ever Change	10
Don't Let Me Down	10
Don't Pass Me By	04
Drive My Car	12
Early in the Morning	29
Eight Days a Week	29
Eleanor Rigby	10
Every Little Thing	02
Everybody's Got Something to Hide Except Me and My Monkey	10
Everybody's Trying to Be My Baby	07
Falling in Love Again	19
Fixing a Hole	28
Flying	16
For No One	10
For You Blue	23
Free As a Bird	02
From Me to You	30
From Us to You	18
Get Back	21
Getting Better	06
Girl	02
Glad All Over	05
Glass Onion	02
Golden Slumbers	01
Goodbye	16
Good Day Sunshine	29

Good Morning Good Morning	03
Good Night	26
Got to Get You into My Life	30
Hallelujah, I Love Her So	27
Happiness Is a Warm Gun	13
Happy Birthday Dear Saturday Club	25
Heather	10
Hello Little Girl	30
Hello, Goodbye	02
Help!	07
Helter Skelter	02
Her Majesty	18
Here Comes the Sun	08
Here, There and Everywhere	03
Hey Bulldog	10
Hey Jude	20
Hold Me Tight	07
Honey Don't	06
Honey Pie	21
How Do You Do It	25
I Am the Walrus	07
I Call Your Name	28
I Don't Want to Spoil the Party	22
I Feel Fine	29
I Forgot to Remember to Forget	12
I Got a Woman	14
I Got to Find My Baby	25
I Just Don't Understand	29
I Lost My Little Girl	28
I Me Mine	09
I Need You	28

I Remember You	18
I Saw Her Standing There	02
I Should Have Known Better	28
I Wanna Be Your Man	22
I Want to Hold Your Hand	02
I Want to Tell You	27
I Want You	14
I Will	30
I Wish I Could Shimmy Like My Sister Kate	25
I'll Be Back	15
I'll Be on My Way	12
I'll Cry Instead	28
I'll Follow the Sun	09
I'll Get You	15
I'm a Loser	29
I'm Down	28
I'm Gonna Sit Right Down and Cry	28
I'm Happy Just to Dance with You	19
I'm Looking Through You	28
I'm Only Sleeping	01
I'm So Tired	29
I'm Talking About You	23
I've Got a Feeling	21
I've Just Seen a Face	01
If I Fell	07
If I Needed Someone	30
If You've Got Trouble	16
In My Life	01
In Spite Of All the Danger	07
It Won't Be Long	06
It's All Too Much	02

It's Only Love	16
Johnny B. Goode	25
Julia	21
Junk	29
Kansas City	04
Keep Your Hands Off My Baby	11
Komm, Gib Mir Deine Hand	24
Lady Madonna	20
Leave My Kitten Alone	10
Lend Me Your Comb	16
Let It Be	06
Like Dreamers Do	28
Little Child	02
Little Queenie	21
Lonesome Tears in My Eyes	28
Long Tall Sally	19
Long, Long, Long	24
Love of the Loved	07
Love Me Do	08
Love You To	22
Lovely Rita	07
Lucille	19
Lucy in the Sky with Diamonds	17
Madman	27
Maggie Mae	22
Magical Mystery Tour	07
Mailman, Bring Me No More Blues	29
March of the Meanies	08
Martha My Dear	21
Matchbox	06
Maxwell's Silver Hammer	24

Mean Mr. Mustard	15
Memphis, Tennessee	23
Michelle	05
Misery	01
Money	16
Moonlight Bay	17
Mother Nature's Son	10
Mr. Moonlight	22
My Bonnie	16
No Reply	02
Norwegian Wood	07
Not A Second Time	01
Not Guilty	19
Nothin' Shakin'	13
Now and Then	30
Nowhere Man	30
Ob-La-Di, Ob-La-Da	02
Octopus's Garden	16
Oh! Darling	07
Old Brown Shoe	04
One After 909	10
One and One Is Two	10
Only a Northern Song	17
Ooh! My Soul	22
Paperback Writer	01
Penny Lane	27
Pepperland	06
Pepperland Laid Waste	07
Piggies	12
Please Mister Postman	29
Please Please Me	07

Polythene Pam	20
P.S. I Love You	30
Rain	28
Real Love	08
Reminiscing	27
Revolution	14
Revolution 1	14
Revolution 9	14
Rip It Up	29
Rock and Roll Music	22
Rocky Raccoon	20
Roll Over Beethoven	05
Run for Your Life	01
Savoy Truffle	08
Sea of Holes	07
Sea of Monsters	07
Sea of Time	07
Searchin'	16
September in the Rain	06
Sexy Sadie	23
Shake, Rattle and Roll	25
Sgt. Pepper's Lonely Hearts Club Band	18
She Came in Through the Bathroom Window	28
She Loves You	06
She Said She Said	25
She's a Woman	08
She's Leaving Home	03
Shout	29
Sie Liebt Dich	24
Slow Down	02
So How Come	13

Soldier of Love	21
Some Other Guy	25
Something	01
Sour Milk Sea	07
Step Inside Love	03
Strawberry Fields Forever	03
Sun King	08
Sure to Fall	25
Sweet Little Sixteen	25
Sweet Georgia Brown	25
Take Good Care of My Baby	10
Take Out Some Insurance on Me Baby	14
Taxman	29
Teddy Boy	05
Tell Me What You See	01
Tell Me Why	07
Thank You Girl	02
That Means a Lot	26
That'll Be the Day	07
That's All Right	12
The Ballad of John and Yoko	24
The Continuing Story of Bungalow Bill	05
The End	30
The Fool on the Hill	08
The Hippy Hippy Shake	19
The Honeymoon Song	25
The Inner Light	03
The Long and Winding Road	06
The Night Before	28
The Palace of the King of the Birds	06
The Sheik Of Araby	06

The Walk	20
The Word	06
There's a Place	30
Things We Said Today	27
Think for Yourself	19
This Boy	30
Three Cool Cats	06
Ticket to Ride	15
Till There Was You	30
Tip of My Tongue	27
To Know Her Is to Love Her	27
Tomorrow Never Knows	30
Too Much Monkey Business	06
Twist and Shout	19
Two of Us	02
Wait	01
Watching Rainbows	13
We Can Work It Out	28
What Goes On	27
What You're Doing	07
What's the New Mary Jane	25
When I Get Home	02
When I'm Sixty-Four	21
Where Have You Been All My Life	09
While My Guitar Gently Weeps	29
Why Don't We Do It in the Road?	10
Wild Honey Pie	21
With a Little Help From My Friends	30
Within You Without You	03
Words of Love	02
Yellow Submarine	06

Yellow Submarine in Pepperland	07
Yer Blues	29
Yes It Is	30
Yesterday	28
You Can't Do That	14
You Know My Name	18
You Know What to Do	16
You Like Me Too Much	24
You Never Give Me Your Money	20
You Really Got a Hold on Me	02
You Won't See Me	30
You'll Be Mine	14
You're Going to Lose That Girl	27
You've Got to Hide Your Love Away	26
Young Blood	05
Your Feet's Too Big	27
Your Mother Should Know	22

Chapter Two
    Ringo–Ginor
    George–Roggee
    John–Hojn
    Paul–Ulap
    Beatlefan–Fantebela

With a Little Help from My Friends

Some Thought to be the Fifth Beatle: Wives and Some Girlfriends

Chapter Thirteen
 Jimmie Nicol–Mimjie

Chapter Fourteen
 Derek Taylor–Keder
 George Martin–Nitmar
 Eric Clapton–Cire

Chapter Fifteen
 Pete Best–Tepe
 Olivia Harrison–Liavio

Chapter Seventeen
 Mal Evans–Lam
 Klaus Voormann–Slauk

Chapter Nineteen
 Linda Mccartney–Dalni

Chapter Twenty
 Maureen Starkey-Reemuna
 Stuart Sutcliffe-Tustar
 Astrid Kirchher-Tridsa

Chapter-Twenty-One
 Cynthia Lennon–Nichaty
 Billy Preston–Libly
 Tony Sheridan–Nyot
 Barbara Starkey–Rabbara
 Nancy Mccartney–Cynan

Chapter Twenty-Two
 Neil Aspinall–Enil

Chapter Twenty-Three
 Yoko Lennon–Koyo
 Brian Epstein–Rabni

Chapter Twenty-Four
 Pattie Boyd–Tepita

Chapter Twenty-Five
 Bruno Koschiider–Nubro
 Murray The K–Rumyar

Chapter Twenty-Six
 Jane Asher–Neja
 Heather Mills–Ratheeh
 May Pang-Mya

About the Author

CAROLYN ADDIE RESIDES ON THE NORTH SHORE of Long Island, New York, where she grew up with her parents and three siblings. After marriage and five children, she began a career in the business management field and is now retired. She is the proud grandmother of five wonderful grandchildren who inspire her creativity. Carolyn loves music and reading, but her true passion is writing.

After retiring, she decided to focus her energy on a novel idea she had many years ago. Thousands of books have been written about The Beatles over the years, but her fifty-year-old idea remains the first of its kind to be released to pay homage to her all-time favorite band. While over three hundred Fab Four song titles are thoughtfully interwoven throughout the book, the story is not about them! It is instead a heartwarming, adventurous fairytale inspired by their lyrics and melodies together with some high-spirited and loving characters. At last, this devoted paperback writer is overjoyed to present her labor of love.

Lightning Source UK Ltd.
Milton Keynes UK
UKHW052328031122
411520UK00011B/223